Gabriel doesn't like his life. It's better than the one he would have if the Gillham pack hadn't rescued him from the streets, but he's working himself to the bone to make sure Alice, the woman he considers his sister, gets better opportunities than him. He realized something was eventually going to break a while ago, but he never expected that the reason for it would be his mate.

Cyn is leaving behind the life he's known until now — including his parents' money, the job they'd been planning for him, and the arranged marriage they want him to enter. He doesn't know what he'll encounter when he goes to Gillham to find his cousin Noah, but it's not a cute shifter telling him they're mates. He never expected to have one, since demons don't have mates, but it's a perfect way to turn his life around.

If only his mate's sister didn't hate him.

This book is a work of fiction. Names, characters, places, and incidents either are products of the author's imagination or are used fictitiously. Any resemblance to actual events or locales or persons, living or dead, is entirely coincidental.

Gabriel
Copyright © 2019 Catherine Lievens
ISBN: 978-1-4874-2655-2
Cover art by Angela Waters

Published by eXtasy Books Inc or
Devine Destinies, an imprint of eXtasy Books Inc

Look for us online at:
www.eXtasybooks.com or www.devinedestinies.com

GABRIEL
WYOMING SHIFTERS: 12 YEARS LATER BOOK 9

BY

CATHERINE LIEVENS

CHAPTER ONE

Gabriel couldn't find his second shoe. He had no idea where the thing had disappeared to. He knew he'd taken them both off at the same time, yet there was only one waiting for him by the front door.

"Alice?" he called out, hoping Alice wasn't studying with her earbuds in.

"Yeah?"

"Have you seen my shoe?"

There was a pause, then Alice appeared at the living room arch. "Your shoe? As in, one of them?"

Gabriel held up the orphan shoe he was holding. "Yes. I only found one."

Alice rolled her eyes. "I swear, you'd lose your head if it wasn't attached to your body." She came closer and poked at the small mountain of shoes on the floor. "You could wear another pair."

Gabriel sighed. "I could, but these are the most comfortable ones, and I have a shift at the shelter."

He recognized the fleeting expression on Alice's face, but he didn't try to reassure her or to change the way she thought about him having two jobs. He'd already tried lots of times, but nothing he said made her feel better about it.

"Gabriel," she started.

"Nope. I don't want to fight tonight, not when I'm almost late. And I *will* be late if I don't find my shoe."

Alice huffed. "You wouldn't be late anywhere if you didn't have to work two jobs."

Gabriel groaned. "There we go again."

"I'm just saying that I could ask Kam to lend me money for college. You don't have to pay for it. You *shouldn't* have to." She leaned down, pushed aside a few shoes, and grabbed the one Gabriel had been looking for. She offered it to him, dangling from her finger.

Gabriel snatched it and sat on the floor to put it on. "I don't *have* to do anything. I'm happy to pay for your college." As much as he could, anyway. Luckily for him, she had a scholarship, but he was still paying back the pack for lending him money so he could go. He wouldn't let Alice indebt herself to anyone, not even to the pack that had taken them in and welcomed them when they'd been teenagers.

Alice glared. "What I meant is that Kameron told you he didn't expect you to pay anything back even if you took the money from him. The pack looks out for its members, and that includes us."

Gabriel knew that. Several of their friends had gone to college on the pack's dime, and no one had found that strange. It wasn't, not when they'd all lived with the pack most of their lives. Of course other street kids had ended up in Gillham, and they'd taken the money, too, but Gabriel had never felt comfortable doing it. He wasn't sure why, but that didn't matter. He was in debt, but Alice didn't have to be.

He got up. "I need to go. I don't want to be late."

Alice glared. "This conversation isn't over, Gabe."

"Is it ever?" She'd been trying to convince him to stop paying for her since her first year in college. She was almost done now — late, because she and Gabriel had needed to recuperate from the years they'd spent on the streets — but some day she'd be a doctor, and Gabriel couldn't have been prouder.

He kissed her cheek, grabbed his bag, and rushed toward the door before she could add anything. He didn't want to fight with her, and that was always how this kind of conversation ended. He didn't like fighting with her. She was his only family, even though they'd both lived with foster parents when they'd arrived in Gillham. Gabriel loved them, but he felt nowhere near as close to them as he felt to Alice, no doubt thanks to the year they'd spent together on the streets.

He rushed to his car. He was almost late, and that meant he wouldn't be able to stop by the coffee shop to get his fuel for the night. The coffee at the shelter wasn't terrible, but it also wasn't his beloved caramel macchiato. It would have to do, though, because Gabriel didn't like being late, which was something that happened fairly often because of how forgetful he was.

He parked in the parking lot, looked forlornly at Gillham Java for a second, then rushed through the back door.

He was late.

Oliver was grinning like an idiot when Gabriel barreled through the door. He checked his watch, and his smile widened. "You almost made it."

Gabriel flipped him the bird and headed toward the office. The room was tiny, but it was enough for a desk and a few chairs. Gabriel dumped his backpack into his chair and scowled at his friend. "What do you want?"

Oliver was still smiling. "Only five minutes. What happened? Did a deer decide to commit suicide in front of your car again?"

"That would have made me more than five minutes late." In fact, the last time that had happened, Gabriel had been two hours late. He didn't like to think about that day, though. "Why are you here and not out there working?"

"I'm going. I'm going. I just wanted to make sure you were okay."

That mollified Gabriel. He and Alice were a unit, a family, but Gabriel also considered Oliver family, albeit in a different way. The three of them and a few others had stayed with the same foster parents at the same time, so they'd spent a few years in close quarters. Some would say that made them siblings, and it did, in a way, but Gabriel's relationship with Alice was always going to be stronger, given the year they'd spent living on the streets together, protecting each other and being each other's world. Nothing was ever going to come close to that kind of bond.

"What was it, then? A duckling crossing?"

That had happened, too, but it was normal. The town of Gillham was fairly large, but it was also located in a forested area. There were a lot of animals around. "Don't you have something better to do than bugging me, *Olivier*?" Gabriel asked.

Oliver's eyes narrowed. "I told you not to call me that."

"You did, and I told you not to bring up all the reasons I've ever been late every time I'm late." Oliver's real name, the one his parents had given him, was Olivier, but he didn't like it. He hated that a lot of people butchered it and thought he was a preppy French man because of it.

Gabriel loved teasing him about it, just like Oliver loved teasing Gabriel about being late.

Oliver rolled his eyes. "Are you going to help out there tonight?"

"As soon as I'm done here." Oliver was a volunteer at the shelter, but Gabriel was being paid to make sure the place ran smoothly. He was the one who accepted donations, who bought the food and the clothes that were needed, who kept an eye on the volunteers and made sure the rent was paid on time. It was a good job, and he liked feeling like he was helping, but he still wished he could be a volunteer and nothing more sometimes. On top of his job at the library, this was exhausting.

Oliver grimaced. "Right. Better you than me."

"We all know how much you hate paperwork."

"I'm pretty sure everyone hates paperwork. Anyway, I'm going. Luke is manning the kitchen right now, but people are going to start arriving, so he's going to need help."

"Go give it to him, then."

Gabriel waited until Oliver was gone to push his backpack onto the floor and flop into his chair. His eyes felt gritty, and he knew it was because he wasn't getting enough sleep. He couldn't wait for the weekend, even though he was so used to getting up at seven in the morning that he ended up doing so even on Saturday and Sunday. At least he could stay in bed those days, even if he was awake.

He grunted and sat up. He needed to stop feeling sorry for himself and get to work. The town had hired him to do this job, and they'd been good enough to allow him to work during the evening when the shelter was open, because they knew about his job at the library.

He wasn't going to disappoint anyone, least of all himself, by being lazy.

"I don't want to go." Cyn was aware of the fact that he sounded like a spoiled toddler, but that didn't change the fact that he didn't want to go to college, and that he *wasn't* going to go, whatever his parents said.

His mother glowered at him. "And what do you want to do, then?"

"I don't know." Except he did, but he knew his parents would never let him. He didn't see why he should waste years of his life studying things he didn't care about when he could get the job he wanted without it.

He'd always loved working on cars, even though his parents would have forbidden it if they'd known. He'd been lucky his parents' driver was a kind man who'd taught him everything he knew about cars. Cyn had been helping him with the cars that belonged to his family since he was fourteen, and he wanted to make a living out of it.

His parents would be scandalized if they knew.

Cyn's family was wealthy, disgustingly so. He was aware of the fact that he'd been lucky to be born there, but that didn't mean he was free to do what he wanted with his life. No, the money and comfort came with chains, and he'd had enough of them, even though he was only nineteen. His parents expected him to go to college and study law like his father had done, then to work with him at his firm. They expected him to marry a suitable woman and have at least two children with her. They expected him to be respectful and bow to their will.

There was no way in hell he was going to do that.

He knew what was going to happen if he told them that, and he was ready to face the consequences, even though he'd thought he'd have more time. He hadn't yet contacted his cousin, but he hoped Noah would still have a place for him, at least until he got his feet under him. He'd been squirreling money away for the past three years, and he probably had enough for an apartment, but he wasn't sure. He had no idea how much an apartment would cost. He had a driver's license, because he'd gotten it without his parents' knowledge, but he didn't have a car. He had no clue how to live without having someone buying his groceries, cooking for him, and doing his laundry.

It looked like he was going to find out sooner rather than later.

"You don't know," his father said. His voice was steady, but Cyn knew how angry his father was. Both his parents were, because he was deigning to defy them, and they hadn't raised him that way.

To be fair, he probably wouldn't be doing this if Noah hadn't walked that path first. The last time Cyn had seen him, he'd only been six, but his mother liked to remind him that he'd end up like his cousin if he didn't listen to her. Cyn didn't know much about Noah's life away from the demon town where he lived and where Noah used to live, but he did know that Noah was mated to a shifter and that he was part of the Gillham pack.

Hopefully, Noah would help him. If he didn't, well, Cyn would find a way. He wasn't going to live the life his parents had planned for him, not when he could live the life he wanted for himself.

"Look, not everyone has to go to college," Cyn tried even though he already knew the kind of answer he'd get.

"And what do you think you can obtain without college? You just said you don't know what you want to do. Can't you figure it out while you're studying?"

Cyn gritted his teeth. Maybe he should tell them about his dream of being a mechanic after all. "I don't want to spend years on books only to find out that I could have done my dream job even without them."

"Your dream job." Cyn's father looked like his head was about to explode. "Do you think that being a lawyer was my *dream job*?"

"I don't know." Did his father even have dreams?

"It wasn't, but my father would have kicked me out if I hadn't done it. I wouldn't have been able to marry your mother, because who would want someone working a job that doesn't require extensive knowledge? Do you realize the kind of doors you are closing by saying *no* to college?"

"I've thought about it, Dad. Besides, I can go to college if I realize I want that." But Cyn was a hundred percent sure he wasn't going to.

"You don't want to go to college?" Cyn's mother intervened.

"I told you. I don't."

7

"All right. That means there's no reason to delay your wedding."

Shit. Cyn hadn't thought about that. His parents wanted him to get married and have children, but they hadn't pushed because he was young and needed to go to college and start working for his father first. But if he didn't go to college, there wasn't a reason not to get married now, or at least, there wasn't a reason as far as his parents were concerned. Cyn had plenty of motives not to want to get married — he didn't want a marriage arranged by his parents, he didn't want to marry a woman because he was really fucking gay, he had no intention of sticking around town, and he didn't want anything keeping him there. He wished his parents were more open-minded, but he hadn't actually expected them to be. He was ready to go, and that was what he would do.

He straightened his back. "I'm not going to get married."

"You're going to do what you're told, Cynara."

"I'm gay. I don't want to marry a woman. I don't want to marry someone you will choose. I want to live my life the way *I* want it, not the way you decide is the right one."

"And how are you going to do that without the family money?" Cyn's father asked. "You're so used to all this that you have no idea how to live without it."

Cyn couldn't deny things were going to be rough in the beginning. He knew they would be, and he'd tried to prepare as much as he could. He hadn't been able to contact Noah, but he knew where Noah lived, and that was where he was going to go as soon as he left here. "I'll learn."

His father scoffed. "You won't be able to. You have money in your veins, Cynara. You were born into it. You'll come back with your tail between your legs in a week."

Cyn rose from the couch. "I won't, but you're free to believe it anyway. I don't want to leave you, because I love you, but I also don't want to let the two of you make a puppet out of me." Sometimes, Cyn wasn't even sure *why* he loved them.

They were his parents, but birthing a child didn't make them a father and a mother. They'd given Cyn money and a house, but it had never been a home. They'd never been loving. Cyn couldn't remember the last time anyone had hugged him, or the last time his mother had kissed him. Sometimes he doubted that had ever happened. Instead, his parents had forced his hand his entire life, pushing him to do things he didn't want, insulting him and berating him when what he did wasn't up to their standards—which was all the time. They'd wanted a perfect puppet child, but instead, they'd gotten Cyn, and they hadn't been happy with that. They'd tried to mold him, but they'd failed, and it was time for Cyn to be free.

"You aren't a puppet. You are our son, and you should behave like it," his mother snapped. "Where is your respect for us?"

"Respect is one thing. Compliance is another." And Cyn wasn't sure he respected them to begin with. "I'm sorry I can't be what you need. I'll leave."

Cyn's father got up. "You won't get another penny from me if you set foot outside this house," he threatened.

Cyn had expected that, and he'd made sure his father couldn't touch the money he'd been putting aside. "I'm sorry," he repeated.

He had to ignore his parents' yells as he headed upstairs to grab the bags he'd packed earlier. He wasn't ever coming back. His parents wouldn't allow it, and he wouldn't have wanted to even if they had.

Gabriel's eyes felt so dry that he was seriously thinking about gouging them. Maybe he could throw them in the sink and hydrate them or something. Anything would feel better than the way he was feeling now.

"Did you get the license plate of the truck that hit you?" Oliver asked from the open door.

Gabriel blinked. "What?"

"You look like shit, and you didn't come to help with dinner."

"Shit." Gabriel checked the time, and sure enough, it was almost eleven PM. "I'm sorry. I was checking the budget, and—"

Oliver raised a hand. "It's fine. We made do without you, don't worry."

"You should have come to get me."

"Luke and I both knew you were working, and that you're probably exhausted. What time did you leave the library today?"

"Uh, six, I think? It was story time this afternoon, and the kids always leave a bit of a mess."

"So you went home, freshened up, and came here. Did you even eat dinner?"

"I had a sandwich. You don't have to worry about me, Ollie. I'm an adult." Hell, Gabriel would hit thirty this year. He mostly still felt like the terrified kid who'd arrived in Gillham almost thirteen years ago, even though he wasn't anymore.

"I know I don't have to. Doesn't mean I'm not going to, and I'm not the only one. What does Alice think of your schedule?"

"She's not happy." Oliver was going to find out anyway. He and Alice were friends. The five of them—Gabriel, Alice, Oliver, Maddox, and Lilah. They'd spent the last years of their teenage period living in the same house, and they were close. Some of them more than others, but that didn't change the fact that they all stuck their noses in each other's business.

"She tried to get you to quit again?"

"Not yet, but she's going to." Gabriel saved the sheet he'd

been working on and turned the computer off. The budget could wait until tomorrow.

"Of course she is, and she's not wrong. I don't get why you don't want Kam to pay for her education like he did with the rest of us."

"She's my responsibility." And nothing was going to change that. "How are things in the kitchen? Is there something I can help you with?"

"Nah. We cleaned up and locked the doors. We can go home."

Gabriel smiled. "You need a ride?" Oliver always did. He owned a bike, but he knew Gabriel didn't like seeing him on that death trap, so he didn't usually use it when he volunteered at the shelter.

Oliver grinned. "Yeah, but I'm driving. You look like you're going to go headfirst into a ditch because you'll fall asleep at the wheel."

"You don't have to do that." Even though it was true that Gabriel felt like he might fall asleep any second.

"I know. I'll sleep on your couch, yeah? That way Alice and I can catch up tomorrow morning. You can drive me back to town when you go to work."

Gabriel knew it was more for his benefit than because Ollie wanted to catch up with Alice, but he was grateful. He always felt like he didn't have enough time to spend with his friends. He was always busy with work, and when he wasn't, he was sleeping.

"Come on, Gabe. Let's go home. I'm sure Alice left you dinner."

"I'm not sharing," Gabriel grumbled even though they both knew he would. Hell, Oliver had probably called Alice to let her know he was coming. She'd had the time to cook for three rather than two.

"You're a mean, mean man."

They met Luke at the back door and left together. Gabriel was the one in charge of locking up, so he did that while Oliver and Luke talked. Then Luke waved goodbye and headed home to his mate while Gabriel trudged to his car. He was grateful Oliver had volunteered to drive. Right now, sleeping in the shelter's parking lot sounded good, and Gabriel wasn't sure he'd be able to stay awake until they were home. He was going to try, of course—he didn't want Oliver to have to be on his own for the ride, even though the house was only ten minutes away. It would be a lousy way to thank him.

"You know you can call me if you need anything," Oliver said once they were in the car.

"I know."

"Including money."

"I'm not asking you for a loan. I don't *need* a loan. I like both my jobs."

"I realize that. I'm just saying that if you finally stopped being pigheaded and accepted Kam's help like we all did, you could quit your job at the shelter but stay on as a volunteer. You wouldn't have to think about budgets and locking up and all that stuff. You'd be free to focus on the *helping people* part."

Gabriel wanted that so very much, but he couldn't have it. Alice was his family, his sister in all but blood, and he was supposed to take care of her and provide for her. The fact that she was twenty-six didn't change that, and neither did knowing that the pack could afford to send her to college ten times over. It was a question of principles, no matter how stupid it sounded right now and how much Gabriel wanted to give in.

"You're not going to do it, are you?" Oliver asked. He sounded resigned. He knew Gabriel well enough to know his answer already.

"I can't."

"Whatever, man. You totally can, but I'm not going to

push. God knows that's not going to help. You're as stubborn as a mule. You're sure you're a skunk shifter?"

Gabriel lightly slapped Oliver's arm. "Shut it."

"You *need* time off, Gabe. You can't continue like this. You're going to collapse, and no one here wants that, least of all you. Who's gonna work your two jobs if you're not able to do it?"

"Can we not talk about this?"

Oliver sighed. "Yeah. It's not like I'm gonna change your mind anyway."

"I wish I could."

"Me too. I mean, I get why you're doing it, why you think that way. I do. I might not have been through what you and Alice went through, but my parents kicked me out, too. I didn't spend as long on the streets as you guys, but that doesn't mean I don't feel like I owe the pack everything I have now. I wouldn't have the shop without Kam. I wouldn't have anything. Hell, I'd probably be dead, and I have no idea how I can ever pay Kameron back. But maybe I don't *have* to pay him back, not in money."

"Ollie —" Gabriel knew what his friend was getting at, but they'd already been over this, and they didn't think the same way.

"You're useful to the pack and the town. You work at the library. You work at the shelter. That's more than enough for Kam, and you know it. He's paid for all us kids' college if we wanted to go. He invested in my bike shop. In return, he expects me to be a good pack member and to help when he needs me. I know he's a good guy and that he's not going to force me to do something I don't want to do or to hold this over my head forever."

"Come on, Ollie. You said we could stop talking about it."

"We will. I just want to say one more thing."

Gabriel sighed. "I'm listening."

13

"Taking his money without paying it back wouldn't be taking advantage of him or the pack. Kameron puts that money aside for this purpose. He wants to take care of us because he's a good alpha, and we're his pack members. That's *literally* his job, and you're not allowing him to do that. You need to stop being a martyr and start living a little, and that's not going to happen if you spend more than twelve hours working every day."

Gabriel couldn't deny anything Oliver had said. He was right, and Kameron had tried to make Gabriel see that more than once. Gabriel didn't seem to be able to let go of the feeling that he owed Kameron this and much more, though—of the feeling that if he didn't pay what he owed back, Kameron was going to kick him and Alice out, and they'd be once again alone in the world.

Cyn needed to hurry before his parents did something drastic to make sure he didn't leave. He rushed upstairs to his bedroom, and after looking around one last time and shoving his feet into his favorite pair of shoes, he grabbed the backpack he'd left on the bed and the big bag he used when he traveled during weekends and went back downstairs.

He'd half expected his parents to be in the entrance waiting for him, but they were still in the living room. He could hear them talking about him and what they should do, and his stomach churned.

"We need to make sure he can't leave the house," his mother said.

"He's not going to. He's too used to being comfortable and not having to work for anything in his life," his father answered.

"That's not going to be enough. You remember my sister's son."

"Noah met his mate. That's the main reason he left. Besides, your sister's husband stepped in and told Noah to live his life the way he wanted it. If he'd stood his ground, Noah would be at home right now, with his wife and their children. I never liked that man."

Cyn almost snorted, but he didn't want them to hear him. He snuck to the back of the house where the kitchen was. The cook was probably in her room, which was a good thing, since she probably would have told Cyn's parents that he was sneaking out again. He quietly opened the back door and slipped out, making sure it was closed before rushing to the garage.

Anton, the driver, lived in the apartment above the garage. Cyn had never been there, since he and Anton usually met in the garage, but he wanted to say goodbye quickly. He'd used the app on his phone to get a Nix, and they would be arriving in five minutes wherever he was, since he'd sent a picture of himself along with the time.

Anton blinked when he opened his door and saw Cyn there. Cyn had had a tiny crush on the man when he was younger — Anton was hot in a silver fox kind of way, with his graying dark hair and the stubble on his square jaw. He was every gay boy's dream, and he'd been Cyn's dream, too, for a while. Not anymore, though. Cyn wasn't letting anything keep him back, not even Anton's hotness.

"What are you doing here?" Anton asked. He looked around, as if he expected Cyn's father to pop up from the bushes on the ground.

"I wanted to say goodbye."

"Goodbye? What are you talking about, Cyn? What did you do?"

"I'm leaving." Cyn's phone pinged, telling him that the Nix was shimmering to him. "I don't want to go to college or marry a woman my parents will pick. I want to become a mechanic."

Anton sighed. "I hope you know what you're doing, kid."

"I do. Trust me. I thought about it long enough."

The Nix shimmered behind Cyn. Cyn caught the movement with the corner of his eye and turned to smile at her awkwardly. "I'll be right there."

She nodded, and Cyn turned back to Anton. "Stay safe."

"I should be the one telling you that. I won't tell your folks I saw you tonight, but you know they're going to try to find a way to get to you."

"I know. Goodbye." Cyn quickly hugged Anton—something he'd never done before—and went to stand in front of the Nix.

"Where to?" she asked.

"The Gillham pack."

"Do you have a precise spot in mind?"

"No. Just the entrance, please." Cyn wasn't about to have her shimmer him into Noah's living room. He didn't even know if Noah would recognize him, and he wanted to stay on his cousin's good side.

The Nix nodded. Cyn put his hand on her forearm, and with one last glance toward Anton, the world as he knew it disappeared.

It was dark when he reappeared only seconds later. Cyn blinked and tried to orient himself. He dropped his hand, and the Nix left, leaving him alone in what looked like a fucking forest. There was a welcome sign that told him he was indeed at the entrance of pack territory, but he had no idea where to go from there. He was going to have to find out, though.

He might as well start walking.

He followed the road into pack territory. There were no lampposts, but he used the flashlight app on his cell phone to make sure he didn't fall on his face. He had no idea where he was going or if he'd be able to find Noah's house, but that wasn't going to stop him, although he did wish that he'd had the talk with his parents in the morning rather than at night. At least there would have been people around, and he could have asked where to find his cousin. As it was, he doubted he'd see anyone, and if he did, they'd probably think he was a thief or something.

Cyn had been walking for about ten minutes and still had no idea where the fuck he was when he heard a car coming up behind him. The lights illuminated him, and he made sure to stick to the side of the road so the car wouldn't run him over. He turned to face it and stuck his arm out, hoping whoever was driving would see him.

The car stopped.

Cyn breathed out in relief and plastered a smile on his face. He stepped closer to the driver side and leaned down. "Hi."

The man who was looking at him got the window down. "Hey. I don't think I know you."

"You don't. I'm new here."

"Can we help you?"

"I'm looking for Noah's house?"

"Noah, huh?"

The guy couldn't miss the fact that Cyn was a demon, not with Cyn's tail swishing behind him.

Cyn nodded. "Yes. He's my cousin."

"He knows you're coming?"

"Not yet. It was a spur of the moment decision."

"I see." The guy looked at the passenger side, where another man was sitting. The man shrugged, and the first one turned back to Cyn. "Hop in. we'll take you there."

Cyn sighed in relief. "Thank you." He hoped the two weren't serial killers, but he was going to have to take that chance. He could defend himself — probably. He was a qiaran demon and could make stuff explode, but he was too young to have complete or even partial control over that. He tended to make it happen at random, and never when he actually wanted to.

He slid into the back seat and closed the door. "I'm Cynara, but you can call me Cyn."

"I'm Oliver. This is Gabriel."

"You guys are part of the pack?"

"Yep. You're not, though."

"I'm not," Cyn confirmed.

His parents would have a fit if they could see him now, sitting in an old car with two shifters he didn't know. They didn't like shifters. They still thought shifters were animals that needed to be controlled, which was why they stuck to their small demon town, even though Cyn's father had left to go to college. He worked almost exclusively with demons, though, and with humans who could afford his hefty bills. No shifters, ever.

And now there Cyn was, sharing a ride with two of them, hoping to be able to spend time with his cousin and his shifter mate.

Cyn suspected his parents would eventually realize where he'd gone. It would take them a while, because they hadn't seen Noah in almost thirteen years, but they remembered him. They knew he lived with the pack and that he was mated with a shifter. They'd suspect this was where Cyn would go, and they'd try to get him to come home.

Cyn peeked out the window. He couldn't see anything, but he hoped this was his home now. And if it wasn't, he'd have to find another one. Maybe he could get an apartment in town. Noah might not want to see him or to get to know him, but that didn't mean Cyn couldn't stay in Gillham and build himself a home here.

He wanted to. He wanted a place where he could belong and be himself, where no one would expect that he follow their orders. He wanted to be happy.

And this was the first step to get that.

Chapter Two

Gabriel was grumpy, which was the only reason why he was also annoyed with Oliver for stopping to give this guy a ride. Of course they should give him a ride. From the sound of it, he was new in Gillham and had no idea where he was going, which could be dangerous in the dark. Some pack members liked to roam during the night, and some of them were dangerous when they thought they were under attack. Gabriel didn't want to think about what would have happened to this guy if his path had crossed Corbin's. Corbin might be a reformed assassin and had been living with the pack for close to fifteen years, but that didn't mean he took kindly to strangers, and Cyn had been edging too close to the house Corbin shared with his mate.

Cyn settled in the back seat and closed the door. Oliver was grinning, and Gabriel couldn't ignore the small burst of irritation that sparked in him. Had Oliver stopped because he wanted to seduce Cyn? For some reason, that annoyed the hell out of Gabriel and his skunk

Cyn shifted position, and the car filled with his scent. He'd been slightly sweating, no doubt thanks to the walk, and while he didn't stink, the warmth of his body helped diffuse his scent. It hit Gabriel right in the nose—and in the feels, because Cyn was his mate.

Gabriel blinked. He was almost afraid to turn around in his seat to check. Cyn was a demon, so he wouldn't know about it, but Gabriel did, and he had trouble processing it.

He'd thought about meeting his mate for years. He was still

young, especially by shifters' standards, but he'd never had someone like a mate in his life, someone who would be there just for him, support him and be a team with him, help him face the world and deal with it. Alice came the closest to that, but she was different, because Gabriel saw her more like a little sister than an accomplice. Cyn looked young, younger than Gabriel and even Alice, but he was Gabriel's mate, and age didn't mean anything when it came to mates.

"Gabe? You okay? Or did you fall asleep?" Oliver asked. There was a hint of worry in his voice that told Gabriel that he'd probably said his name him a few times already. Gabriel hadn't answered because he was trying to come to terms with, well, everything that had happened and the ramifications of it.

Gabriel worked too much to have a social life. His two jobs meant he wouldn't have much time for Cyn, although of course, the fact that Cyn was his mate didn't mean that Cyn would want anything to do with him.

"Gabe, you're worrying me, because I can see your eyes are open. Do I need to stop the car?" Oliver asked.

Cyn leaned forward, closer to Gabriel, and asked, "Is he okay?"

Gabriel shook himself. "I'm fine. Stop worrying, Ollie."

Oliver snorted. "Stop worrying? You look like you've seen a ghost, although that's probably because you're dead tired, but still. You had me worried for a second. I told you, you need to rest more. Having two jobs is too hard on you, especially jobs that are so demanding."

Gabriel ignored him and twisted in his seat so he could look at Cyn. He was painfully young, and the exoticness of him didn't change that. He blinked big, swirling blue and black eyes at Gabriel and smiled tentatively. Gabriel could see his tail moving behind him, wrapping and unwrapping around his waist as if he wasn't controlling it, and the tiny horns on Cyn's head begged to be touched. Gabriel *wanted* to touch them, so he grabbed the seat and squeezed as hard as he needed to in order to stop thinking inappropriate thoughts. "You said you were looking for Noah?" he asked.

Cyn nodded, sending another wave of his scent toward Gabriel. "Yes. He's my cousin."

"I didn't know he had a cousin."

Cyn grinned. "Are you a friend of his?"

"Not really, but everyone knows everyone here, and everyone's business, of course. There are no secrets when a group of people this small live together."

"I was under the impression that the pack was big."

"It is if you compare it to other packs, but we only have about a hundred and fifty members. A lot more than there were when I first arrived here thirteen years ago, but still a small number when it comes to gossip."

The corner of Cyn's lips curled. "I see. It's not what I'm used to."

"What are you used to?"

Cyn shrugged.

He had a slight frame, and Gabriel wanted to see if he'd fill in over the years. *Jesus.* Just how young was Cyn?

"If you know Noah, you know he comes from money."

Noah had never mentioned anything like that, but everyone in the pack knew it. "I know."

"Our mothers are sisters. Both our families are rich and isolated."

"Too good to mix with commoners?" Oliver asked. He didn't sound angry or offended, but not everyone understood his humor.

Cyn laughed. "Pretty much. They don't like to mix with people they consider inferior, and that doesn't leave a lot of people to be around, you know? Plus they don't like shifters and barely tolerate humans. Let's say I've had a lonely childhood and life."

"And now you're here," Gabriel said. What were the odds that he'd meet his mate today, of all days? Nothing had made it different. Gabriel had gotten no clue that his life would be turned upside down right after work.

Cyn nodded. "Hopefully to stay."

"Yeah? Does that mean that you left home?"

"I did."

He looked too young to be away from his parents, no matter how bad they sounded. *Shit.* Was he even eighteen? Gabriel's heart had grabbed the fact that they were mates and run with it, but Gabriel's brain needed to get into play, too. "No offense, but you look way too young to be on your own."

Oliver made a strangled sound, but Gabriel ignored him. He realized they'd both already been on their own several years by the time they'd turned eighteen, but that had been different. They hadn't chosen to leave their families. They'd been forced to.

Cyn arched a perfect brow. "I'm nineteen. I know it's young, but that doesn't mean I can't live on my own. Plenty of people my age do."

Gabriel sagged in relief. His mate was legal. "You're right, they do. But from what you said, your new life here is going to be very different from what you're used to."

Cyn frowned. "I'm aware of that. I might be only nineteen, but that doesn't mean I haven't thought about all this."

"We're here," Oliver interrupted.

Gabriel wanted more time to talk to Cyn, but now probably wasn't the right moment to tell him they were mates.

He scrambled out of the car to help Cyn with his two bags, ignoring the puzzled, and at the same time, amused look on Oliver's face. "Do you need me to carry this to the door?" Gabriel asked.

"No, thank you." Cyn smiled. "I don't know how to thank

you for your help today."

"You don't have to. You're about to become a pack member, and we look after each other. Actually, why don't you give me your number? I'll text you so you have mine, and you can let me know if you need anything." Gabriel heard Oliver guffaw from the open window of the car, but he resisted the urge to flip him the bird.

"I didn't think you'd ask."

Gabriel had to scramble to get his phone out of his pocket. Cyn recited his number, and Gabriel's heart pounded along with the numbers. He hoped Cyn wouldn't be angry at him for not telling him about them right away, but he suspected Cyn had bigger things to focus on right now. Gabriel wasn't going anywhere. He'd be there when Cyn was ready to talk or when he *needed* to. He'd be there to support him through whatever he was going through.

It felt weird to already care for Cyn so much, but Gabriel knew it was the bond, and that the need would become even stronger as time passed, and later, once they bonded.

Jesus. This was actually happening, wasn't it?

Cyn waited until the car was gone to turn toward the house. He had no idea what to expect, but his first experience with Gillham pack members had been a good one. He hoped things would go as well with Noah and his mate as they'd gone with Gabriel and Oliver. He'd liked both of them, but especially Gabriel. Gabriel was cute and apparently interested, and Cyn hoped he'd have the chance to explore whatever that meant.

But first he had to talk to his cousin and try to convince him to let him stay with him, at least until he managed to get his own place.

Cyn swallowed and climbed the porch steps. The house was pretty, but nothing like the one where Noah had lived before. Cyn's mother would be horrified, but Cyn liked it. He didn't need two living rooms and a giant dining room.

He knocked and waited, shuffling on his feet. He was more nervous than he'd been when he'd sat down to talk to his parents earlier, and he couldn't stop himself from swinging his tail. It was a habit his father had wanted him to break, but Cyn hadn't worked on it as much as he should have. Who cared if he swung his tail when he was nervous? He wasn't going to be a lawyer anyway. Besides, it wasn't like his father went to court with his tail out. No, he wrapped it around his waist like most demons in the human world did. No one wanted to be stared at like a circus phenomenon, and they already got enough of that with their eyes and hair. Cyn was glad Gabriel hadn't stared at his face. He knew he was weird-looking from a human or a shifter's point of view, but neither Gabriel nor Oliver had said anything about that or had stared.

The door opened. A man Cyn didn't know stood in front of him, frowning. He had short brown hair and brown eyes and was taller than Cyn—although that wasn't exactly a feat since Cyn had never grown past five foot nine. "Yes?" the man asked.

Cyn rubbed the back of his neck. "Hi. My name is Cynara. I'm looking for my cousin, Noah."

"Your cousin?"

"Yes. I know he lives with the pack, and when I asked for help, someone drove me here. I hope this is his house and not someone else's. If it is, I apologize."

"No, no, Noah does live here. I didn't know he had a cousin, although he doesn't often talk about his family." He stepped to the side. "Come on in. Noah is in his studio. I'll show you the way. Oh, and I'm Duncan, your cousin's mate."

Cyn knew he was some kind of shifter, maybe wolf since they lived with the pack, although Cyn had heard that the Gillham pack was a mixed bunch. "It's a pleasure to meet you." Cyn's voice sounded stiff. He didn't like it, but he tended to revert to being overly polite when he was nervous, and he was fucking nervous. He had no idea what was going to come out of this.

He knew he could find a hotel or something if Noah didn't want to help him. He had more than enough money put aside to stay on his feet even if he floundered. But Noah was family, and right now, Cyn was utterly alone in the world. He didn't like his parents much, but they'd been a constant in his life, and knowing he had no one he could count on was strange and uncomfortable.

He followed Duncan through the house until they reached a door. Duncan knocked but only waited a few seconds before opening the door. He smiled at Cyn as he did so. "Noah tends to get lost in his head when he paints."

Cyn was happy to know that Noah was still painting. He remembered his cousin loved art but also that he hadn't been allowed to create freely.

He stepped in and blinked. The walls of the room were a light cream color, but that wasn't what caught his attention. No, what did were the dozens of canvases leaning against the walls and propped up on an easel.

Cyn didn't know much about art, much to his parents' dismay. He knew what he liked, but more often than not, that meant the art wasn't expensive, not like the paintings that hung on the walls of the house he'd grown up in. He didn't like all of Noah's paintings—he'd never understood modern art, with all its lines and whatnot—but some of them were stunning.

Then there was Noah. He hadn't changed since the last time Cyn had seen him. His blue hair was long and pulled up into a sloppy bun. His tail swung freely behind him, moving along with the music that came from the MP3 player in the corner. There were streaks of color on Noah's cheek, and his clothes and hands were a mess, but he looked happy, and *that* was what Cyn wanted.

He wanted to be happy. He wanted to do things that made him happy, and working on cars did that for him.

"Noah? Your cousin is here," Duncan said. He strode toward Noah and gently touched Noah's back.

Noah jerked, but his brush hadn't been on the canvas, so the painting he was working on was safe. "What?" He blinked and looked around, but Cyn wasn't sure he recognized him, or even that he noticed him. What Duncan had said about Noah losing himself in his head when he painted was obviously true.

"Your cousin."

"My cousin?" Duncan turned Noah toward Cyn.

Cyn wasn't sure what to do, so he raised a hand and waved. "Hi." It sounded stupid, but what did you tell a cousin you hadn't seen in thirteen years when you were hoping he'd give you a room to stay in his house?

Noah frowned. He squinted and stared at Cyn for a moment, then his eyes widened. "Cynara?"

Cyn rubbed the back of his head. "Cyn, but yeah. It's me."

"I haven't seen you since you were a kid."

"I know. I wish—"

"Don't even say it. I'm aware of the reason we didn't see each other since then. It's okay. I'm still surprised to see you here, though."

"Maybe we could move this to the living room?" Duncan suggested. "I could make some tea."

"Coffee?" Noah asked.

"Nope. The last time you had coffee after eight PM, you stayed up half the night to paint. I'm not going to bed alone tonight."

"Right. Come on, Cyn. Let's go talk. I assume you're here for a reason, and I can't wait to hear it."

Cyn was surprised when Noah hooked an arm around his and dragged him along the hallway, but he went along with it. Not everyone was like his parents. He was allowed to hug people, even though it made him uncomfortable and awkward.

"Come on, tell me. Not that I'm not happy to see you, but I have to admit I didn't expect it," Noah said as he dragged Cyn into the living room.

The place was cozy, with pillows on the comfortable used couch. It made Cyn feel at home even though he hadn't yet begged for help. "I left home," he started to explain.

"Is your mother still so similar to mine?"

"Very much so."

Noah flopped onto the couch and grimaced. "I guess I don't have to ask why you left, then."

"I don't want to go to college. I want to be a mechanic. I'm good at it, and I like it. I also don't want to marry whatever girl they have on hand already. They wanted to push for both, and I told them no. They said they'd cut me off and that I had to obey if I wanted to continue living with them."

"And here you are. I'm glad you thought of me when you needed help."

"I wasn't sure you'd be happy to see me."

Noah knocked their shoulders together. "We're family. Of course I'm happy to see you, even though I barely know you. You need a place to stay?"

"Only until I manage to find my own place. I have money set aside, so I hope it won't be long, but more than a room, I, ah, I wanted to know I wasn't alone, you know?"

Noah's expression softened. "Of course. And you're welcome to stay with us, although I should probably ask Duncan about it first. But like I said, you're family. I'm not going to kick you out the way your parents did."

"What was that about?" Oliver asked as soon as Gabriel was back in the car.

Gabriel thought Cyn should probably be the first one to find out they were mates, but he had no idea when he'd see him next, or when he'd be able to talk to him. Besides, Oliver was one of his best friends. He'd be happy for him. "He's my mate," Gabriel blurted out before he could obsess over the decision of telling Oliver or not.

The car swerved. Gabriel grabbed the door handle and held on, shouting, "What the fuck?"

"You can't tell me something like that while I'm driving!" Oliver shouted back.

"Olivier! Eyes back on the road, now!"

Oliver grumbled, but he obeyed. When Gabriel didn't feel like he was having a heart attack again, he let go of the handle and forced himself to relax. "Sorry for startling you. I didn't think you'd take it that way."

"How did you think I'd take it? You just told me the cute little *young* demon we picked up is your mate."

"He's nineteen."

"You're twenty-nine, but you're right, that doesn't matter. He's your mate, and he's legal."

"Do you have to say it like that? It makes me feel like I'm robbing the cradle."

"You kind of are, but okay. So he's your mate, huh?"

"Yeah. I'm not quite sure what to do about it."

"What do you want to do? Did you tell him?"

"Not yet. It's obvious he has his own problems right now, and I don't want to overwhelm him."

"Knowing he's your mate might help, though. It would give him something nice to focus on. But you do you. I don't think I'd be able to keep my mouth shut if I met my mate."

"You're not able to keep your mouth shut ever, Ollie."

Ollie growled and slapped Gabriel's thigh, but he was joking around. They both were — even though it was true that Oliver couldn't keep his mouth shut, as he showed when they got to Gabriel's house, and he blurted, "Gabriel met his mate today," as soon as he saw Alice.

Gabriel groaned while Alice's eyes widened. "Is he joking?" she asked Gabriel. "He has to be joking, right? Because you definitely would have called me if he wasn't."

"I literally met the guy ten minutes ago, Allie. Give me a break, yeah?" Gabriel was bone-tired, but he wasn't sleepy anymore. Meeting one's mate would do that to a person.

"What's his name? Is he from around here? A pack member? Because I think we know pretty much everyone, so that would be weird. Or did you meet him at the shelter?"

Gabriel laughed. He'd been tense, unsure how Alice would take this, but she sounded happy. "Slow down. I can't tell you much since I just met him. His name is Cynara, although he goes by Cyn. He's a demon, Noah's cousin, and he's new in town."

"When are you seeing him again?"

"I have no idea. I gave him my number, and I have his, but that's it for now." And it would probably be better if Gabriel waited until tomorrow to text Cyn. He was so tired that anything he might write would make no sense.

"And he's nineteen," Oliver said as he took his boots off and left them on the pile of shoes that already haunted the entrance.

Alice blinked. "Nineteen? Shit."

Gabriel shrugged. "He's young, but that doesn't mean we can't be together. Besides, it's not like we *are* together. Maybe he'll want to take things slow and be friends before jumping into the bonding thing."

"Bonding? Gabe, he's nineteen. Would you have bonded at nineteen?"

Gabriel would have. He wasn't sure it would have been for the right reasons, but that didn't change the fact that he'd have said yes.

He'd always wanted a family. He had one with Alice and their friends, but it wasn't the same as having a mate. It didn't complete him the way the bond with Cyn would eventually.

"Being young doesn't mean the man is an idiot," Oliver pointed out as they headed to the kitchen. It smelled of roasted chicken, and Gabriel's stomach growled.

"I never said he was an idiot, just that he's young. And it has nothing to do with the ten years of difference, not exactly. But ten years *is* a lot, especially from the point of view of a nineteen-year-old. He probably wants to have fun, while Gabriel wants to settle down."

"You can't know that," Gabriel said. He loved Alice, but did she have to rain on his parade today, of all days? Couldn't she have waited until tomorrow? Gabriel was still riding the high of having met his mate, and she was stomping all over his warm and fuzzy feelings.

"He's right, Al," Oliver intervened. Gabriel could have kissed him.

"I'm not saying he's not, but you don't know anything about the guy. I don't want Gabriel to get hurt because he let his emotions run away."

"I don't need you to protect me or my feelings," Gabriel grumbled.

"And I don't need you to work two jobs so I can afford college, yet you do it."

"It's not the same thing." But they'd been over this often enough for Gabriel to know where she was going with this.

It *was* true that sometimes he tended to treat her like a kid. He'd been protecting her since they'd met on the streets when he was sixteen and she was thirteen. She'd been a slip of a girl running away from her stepfather, and Gabriel had taken her under his wing. He'd already been on the streets for a year by then, so he'd known how things worked, while she'd been so innocent.

He'd kept the habit of taking care of her. It was ingrained in him by now, even though she was twenty-six and had a home and friends. They were both a little overprotective of each other, even though it had been thirteen years since they'd been on the streets. Gabriel didn't know if more time would change that, but if it didn't, life would.

Soon, Alice would graduate and leave for med school, and he'd met Cyn now. Even if they didn't rush into things, they were mates, and there was a good chance that eventually they'd bond and move in together.

Gabriel and Alice were going to have to deal with that and to put some space between each other. Gabriel wasn't sure he liked that thought, but it was time for them to grow up.

She hugged him while Oliver went to the oven to take the chicken out. "I didn't mean to hurt you," she murmured.

"You didn't hurt me. I just wish I'd had more than ten minutes to enjoy the fact that I found my mate."

"Sorry." She kissed Gabriel's cheek. "This is going to change things, isn't it?"

"I was thinking about that. I guess the changes would have happened sooner or later anyway."

"Maybe, but finding your mate is one hell of a way to change your life."

"It is."

"Just—be careful, okay? I know you. You want to throw yourself in this and ignore all the warning signs. I don't know if I'd do things differently if I were in your shoes, but I worry for you. I always will, even when you're mated and we're sixty."

"You'll be married or mated by then, too." Or at least he hoped so. He knew that even though Alice talked tough and insisted she was fine on her own, she yearned for love like he did.

"Nah. But I'll be a world-renowned surgeon, and that's okay with me. I'm not looking for love the way you are. I'm not a romantic."

"Or maybe you're a closet romantic."

"Tell anyone, and I'll kill you."

They both laughed, and it felt like the calm before the storm. Gabriel had no idea what the future held for them, but he knew they'd always be there for each other. Maybe not in the same way, but that was okay. They were growing, like everyone else, and they needed to accept that and deal with whatever life threw at them.

"I love you," he told her.

"Love you, too. And I expect to meet this mate of yours ASAP."

"You don't have to question him. He's my mate."

"Doesn't mean he's good enough for you."

That freaked Gabriel out, because he was pretty sure that for Alice, no one would ever be good enough for him.

Cyn already knew who was calling when his phone started ringing, and he didn't want to answer. He, Duncan, and Noah were still in the living room, talking about what Cyn's plans were. He felt like he'd barely had time to pull away from his parents and they were already trying to reel him back in, and he was probably right. They had to be freaking out right now.

He knew what had happened. They'd talked about what they were going to do. His ungratefulness couldn't be allowed to go unpunished. They were probably going to threaten him to take all his money away again, and if that didn't work, they'd move on to his phone and his computer, as if Cyn were still a child.

He supposed he was, in some ways. He'd been living off his parents' money all his life. The money he'd managed to put aside he'd earned working on cars for friends, and he also had two different accounts where his grandparents had put money. Anything else, anything he'd gotten through his parents, he'd left behind. He'd been careful to use only *his* money in the past few years because he'd already been planning to leave, and he'd known they wouldn't take it well.

"You're not answering?" Noah asked.

Cyn sighed and looked at his phone on the coffee table. At least he'd remembered to turn the sound off. The vibration was annoying, but not enough that he felt he had to answer. "I don't want to."

"Your mother?"

"Probably. She's always the first to call. If she isn't able to convince me, my father tries."

"Are you sure they're not simply worried?" Duncan asked. "You did sneak out without even telling them you were leaving."

Cyn snorted. "Oh, yeah, they're worried all right. What's going to happen if their friends find out they can't even keep me under control? And what about the parents of the girl they want me to marry? They all decided to wait until I graduated from college, but they're going to notice it if I'm not around. I'm supposed to date her for the next few years, show the town that we're getting along and all that crap."

Noah winced. "I remember when my mother tried to set me up. It wasn't fun."

"It still isn't." The phone stopped vibrating, but Cyn knew it was going to start again soon enough. He rubbed his face, feeling tired beyond what should be possible. "I don't want to marry a woman because my parents think she's a good match. I'm gay, very much so."

Cyn's phone started vibrating again. The three of them

looked at it as if it were a snake ready to strike.

"She's going to keep on calling until you answer," Noah pointed out.

"I know. I should turn it off between two calls."

"Or you could answer, tell her you're safe and that you're not coming home, and make it clear to her that if she just wants to berate you and yell at you, she should stop calling."

Noah had more experience with this than Cyn. They'd briefly talked about his parents, and Cyn had been surprised to find out that Noah's father *really* was okay with him being mated to a shifter. Cyn already knew Noah's mother despised it—she came over to his house often enough that he'd heard her lamenting that fact at least once a week since he was seven—but she'd never mentioned the fact that she and her husband thought so differently about it. From what Noah had said, his parents were married in name only by now. Cyn knew better than to hope that at least one of his parents would be supportive, though. With them, it was their way or the highway, and he'd chosen the highway. They knew it, yet they were still trying to change his mind and force him back into the life they demanded he have.

Cyn snatched the phone from the coffee table. Noah was right. Cyn's mother wasn't going to give up, and Cyn didn't want to be afraid every time his phone rang. He might as well answer now and face the music.

"Hello?" he asked.

"Where are you?"

Cyn jumped and pulled the phone away from his ear. His mother rarely yelled, so he knew she was angry. Of course, he'd known that even before leaving the house. She was always angry when he defied her and his father. "I left."

"We saw that, Cynara. I thought we'd been clear. You aren't allowed to leave the house without authorization."

"And I told you that I wasn't going to follow your rules

and marry that girl. Remember it only happened an hour ago."

"How dare you do this?"

"I want to live my life."

"You want to live your life? After all we've done for you, this is how you repay us? We've fed you, clothed you ever since —"

The phone was snatched out of Cyn's hand. He jerked, happy not to be hearing his mother's screams as loud as he had seconds before, and he watched as Noah grinned and put the phone to his ear.

"Hello, Auntie."

That was enough to shut Cyn's mother up. She was no doubt in shock at the sound of Noah's voice. She hadn't heard from him or seen him ever since Noah had left thirteen years ago.

Noah's smile widened. "I just wanted you to know that Cyn is safe. He'll be staying with my mate and me in the Gillham pack territory until he finds an apartment of his own. And before you say it, no, I don't care what you think about that or that you're going to tell my mother. I haven't heard from her in thirteen years, and I doubt this will change her mind. The two of you are so alike, it hurts me to think about it. Anyway, you should leave Cyn alone now. I think he was more than clear about the fact that he has no intention of doing what you and your husband want him to do when it comes to his career and his marriage."

"Goodbye, Auntie. And say hi to my mother for me." Noah said. He handed the phone back to Cyn.

Cyn had no idea what his mother was going to say to him, but he suspected Noah's speech hadn't changed her mind. It would take much more than a few words for that to happen. Cyn wasn't sure anything would ever change his mother's mind, and he was done trying to make her see that happiness was more important than what others thought and money.

"Cynara," she snapped.

"Yes."

"I cannot *believe* you went to your cousin. How could you, after what he did to your aunt?"

"He's free to live his life the way he wants to. He's happy. I want the same things, and you and Father wouldn't let me."

"You will not be welcome back here if you persist in this path."

"I know."

"You will not get one more cent from us. Your father will cancel your credit card first thing tomorrow morning."

"I know, Mother. If that's the price I have to pay to live my life, then I'll pay it. It was never about the money."

"It's *always* about the money. You're going to regret this when you can't afford what you want or when you have to pay rent." She said that as if paying rent was a dirty thing to do, and maybe in her eyes, it was. She'd never had to pay rent. She and Cyn's father had bought the house Cyn had shared with them until now right before they got married. Actually, Cyn's father had bought it, and he'd let her furnish it, as was done. The male took care of everything financial while the female was left with the creative stuff, and no one was allowed to change those roles.

But Noah had. He was a painter, and he was bonded with his mate. He hadn't married the woman his parents had chosen for him, and neither would Cyn.

CHAPTER THREE

Gabriel's palms felt sweaty. He wasn't one to have sweaty hands, but he might be starting to. Nothing had ever made him as nervous as the thought of calling Cyn was right now, and he wasn't sure how to get over it.

Cyn had seemed interested in Gabriel when they'd talked last night, but they'd only been together ten minutes at the most. Maybe he'd changed his mind in the meantime. Maybe he'd realized he shouldn't go for the first guy he met in Gillham. Maybe he didn't want a guy in his life. It was going to take him a while to get used to this new life of his, and it would be easier if he didn't have to keep someone else in mind, too.

And maybe Gabriel was a chicken shit, and he should call and see what Cyn wanted. Cyn might not know that they were mates, but that didn't mean he was going to tell Gabriel to fuck off. They'd gotten along well enough last night, and hopefully, that was a taste of what was to come.

Gabriel snatched his phone from the table and unlocked it. He found Cyn's number, took a deep breath, and pressed it.

It rang. Of course it did. There were no reasons why Cyn should have given Gabriel a fake number.

"Hey, Gabriel!"

Gabriel blinked. Cyn sounded happy to hear from him, which was weird, but good. "Hey, Cyn. Everything okay?"

"Yeah. I was nervous last night, but my cousin and his mate are letting me stay with them. We had a good talk, so they know what's going on."

"Do you want to talk about it?"

"I don't know. I'd rather talk about anything but that, to be honest, but if you want, we can. I'm looking forward to seeing you again."

"You are?" Gabriel knew he probably sounded like an idiot, but he hadn't expected Cyn to be so open about what he was feeling. They didn't know each other yet after all, and Cyn had no idea they were mates. Gabriel was going to have to tell him, and he hoped Cyn wouldn't take it badly.

"I am. You and Oliver were nice last night, and there's a reason I gave you my number, you know."

"I see. Do you want Oliver to be there when we see each other?" Cyn had mentioned both of them, so Gabriel wanted to be sure.

"I'm sure Oliver is a nice guy, but I'd rather see only you. Like I said, I gave *you* my number, right?"

"Right. Uh, are you doing anything right now?" Gabriel had made sure to come home early today. It wasn't even dark outside yet, and he'd asked Oliver to make sure everything ran smoothly at the shelter. He'd also told his boss there that he needed a night off for personal reasons, and luckily for him, she hadn't protested. So for the first time in what felt like forever, Gabriel had the rest of the afternoon and the evening free, and he wanted to spend that time with Cyn. Since it looked like Cyn wanted the same thing, Gabriel hadn't stopped himself from asking if he was free.

He hoped the answer to that would be yes.

"Right now? Nothing, actually. What did you have in mind? I'd ask you to come over, but I live with my cousin and his mate now, and they're very lovey-dovey for people who've been together for thirteen years. I found them going at it on the kitchen table this morning."

Gabriel laughed. "They're not used to having to be careful. You just moved in with them."

"I know. I'm not berating them. I'm grateful they're letting me stay, and you should have heard Noah when my mother called last night. He told her what he thought of her behavior. But anyway, I was trying to say that maybe it would be better if I left for a while so Noah and Duncan can have some Cyn-free time, you know?"

"How about you come to my house? My sister lives with me, but she's studying, so she'll probably stick to her room."

"You have a sister? That's nice. I always wanted siblings, but I doubt my parents had sex more than the one time it took them to have me."

Gabriel spluttered. Did Cyn just say whatever passed through his mind? "I'll text you the directions. It's not far from your cousin's house, maybe five minutes through the forest."

"Good. I've wanted to take a walk since I saw the trees last night."

"You didn't this morning?"

"I couldn't. I spent most of my day dealing with the fallout of leaving home."

"You left home?"

Cyn sighed. "That's part of the things I don't want to talk about, but especially not on the phone. I'll tell you when I get to you, okay? Text me the directions, and I'll be there before you can realize you shouldn't have invited me."

There was no way that was going to happen, but Gabriel didn't say it. Instead, he hung up, texted Cyn, and started freaking out about having him at home. The place was a mess—both he and Alice were naturally messy, but things had gotten bad, what with Gabriel's two jobs and Alice's school.

The sink in the kitchen was overflowing with dirty dishes, there was an empty bottle of water on the table, along with crumpled napkins and crumbs, the trash needed to be taken out — and that was only the kitchen. The entrance still looked like a shoe cemetery, and Gabriel was pretty sure he'd seen a basket of dirty laundry on the stairs when he'd rushed down this morning.

Instead of freaking out, he needed to start working. It wouldn't take more than five minutes for Cyn to get there if he left right away, but he'd probably need some time to get ready, so Gabriel hoped to have fifteen minutes.

He threw away the empty bottles, cleaned the table, and stuck all the dirty dishes into the dishwasher. He was pretty sure they wouldn't come out clean if he started it, but at least they were out of sight. Next, he rushed to the entrance, hid the laundry basket in the closet where they hung their coats, and pushed all the shoes inside. That was where they were supposed to be anyway, but neither he nor Alice ever took the time to do it.

"What are you doing?" Alice asked from the living room. She was on the couch with what had to be half a dozen books and notebooks spread around her. She'd balled up some sheets of paper and had thrown them around, and there were three half empty cups of coffee littering the coffee table.

Gabriel didn't have the time to clean the living room, so he hoped Cyn wouldn't mind talking in the kitchen, or even better, going for a walk. Gabriel wanted Cyn and Alice to meet, but he also wanted to spend time alone with his mate. Besides, Alice was studying, so she probably wouldn't be grateful for the interruption.

"Cyn is coming here."

Alice cocked her head. "You mean right now?"

"Yes."

"I still don't see what it has to do with you running around the house like a mad man."

"I don't want him to think we live in a pigsty. We haven't washed dishes in days, and what's with that laundry basket?

41

The laundry room is upstairs, you know."

"I know. I put all the clothes I found around this floor into it, but I forgot to take it upstairs. And I want to point out that some of those were *your* clothes."

Gabriel took a deep breath. "Sorry. I'm nervous."

"Understandable. "Are you going to tell him he's your mate?"

"I don't know. I guess it depends on how things go."

"You should tell him sooner rather than later. I don't know him, but I wouldn't be happy if my mate kept it to himself. It sucks that he has no other way to find out, and he has a right to know."

"I'm aware of that." That didn't mean the thought of saying those three words wasn't terrifying, though.

A knock on the door made Gabriel's eyes go wide. He looked at Alice, who smiled and shooed him away. "Go. Introduce us, then find something the two of you can do without making too much noise. Or I could go to my room?"

"Stay here. I think we're going to go for a walk." Gabriel didn't want anyone around, just in case Cyn rejected him. He didn't want anyone, not even Alice, to see him at his worst.

Cyn beamed at Gabriel when the door opened. He'd almost gotten lost once, but a quick call to Noah had helped him find his way to Gabriel's home. "Hey. You're like Little Red Riding Hood, huh?"

Gabriel blinked. "What?"

"You live in the middle of the woods, with wolf shifters around. Are you a wolf shifter?" It was too easy to imagine running fingers through Gabriel's fur—wolf *and* human, if he had it in this form.

"Uh, no. I'm a skunk shifter."

Were skunks the ones that stank? Cyn wasn't sure, but he

was going to have to find out. Not that he thought Gabriel would stink him up, but he didn't want to say something stupid or offend Gabriel. "And are you as cute in your skunk form as you are in your human one?" he asked, hoping his flirting wouldn't make Gabriel run away. Not everyone liked it, especially when he was that blatant about it.

Someone in the house — Gabriel's sister, no doubt — laughed.

Gabriel stepped aside. "Why don't you come in? I figured I could introduce you and Alice. Then we could go for a walk or something."

"Sounds good."

A movement to his right made Cyn turn once he was in the entrance. Of *course* Alice was going to be a stunning blonde. She was short, but she had big blue eyes and long blond hair that she'd pulled up into a messy bun. She wasn't wearing makeup, and Cyn could see a smattering of small, faded freckles on her nose and cheekbones.

She looked adorable, and he wanted to kick her out of the house so he could be alone with Gabriel. He wasn't sure why, and he didn't much care. He liked Gabriel, and the fact that he'd never reacted to anyone else the way he was reacting to Gabriel didn't change the way he was going to behave, although he should probably try to curb his murderous instincts.

"This is Alice. We grew up together, since we met when we were teenagers," Gabriel said.

Cyn forced himself to smile. "Hey, Alice. I'm Cyn." He was sure Alice was a nice woman. She hadn't done anything to earn herself the dislike he felt for her, so he made sure none of it showed on his face. He'd been raised not to show what he was feeling, and for once, he was grateful his mother had insisted on that.

"Cyn told me you were new here?"

"I am. I arrived yesterday. I'm staying with my cousin."

"Sounds nice. Why are you here?"

"Alice," Gabriel hissed.

She ignored him and stared at Cyn, waiting for an answer.

Maybe she wasn't such a nice person after all. Cyn wasn't an idiot, and he could hear the slight hostility in her tone. He hadn't done anything to warrant it as far as he knew, and he didn't want to start a fight with her, especially not in front of Gabriel. Maybe they were only friends, or maybe they'd been more once, and Alice was jealous, although why she should be, Cyn didn't know. Maybe she was in love with Gabriel and didn't like that Cyn was encroaching on her territory. Whatever the reason, he wasn't going to be the one starting a war between them.

He beamed at her, enjoying her nonplussed expression. "I left home. Ran away, I guess. My parents wanted me to go to college, and they didn't take it well when I told them I didn't want to go."

"Wait. They wanted you to go, as in, they were going to pay for it?"

"Of course. They can afford it."

"And you said no. Just like that."

"I don't want to go to college, so I don't see why I should do it."

"Do you know how many people would give an arm or a leg to have the opportunity you shit on?"

Cyn blinked.

Gabriel grabbed Alice's arm and leaned close to her. "What are you doing?" he asked, not softly enough for Cyn not to hear.

"You heard him. He could have gone to college without worrying about the price, and he said *no*. In the meantime, you're still paying the pack for your degree, and you're working two jobs to pay for mine."

Gabriel gave Cyn an apologetic smile. "Sorry about that.

We're not as well-off as you, I guess."

Cyn didn't like the thought that Gabriel was working two jobs to send his friend to college, even though she was his best friend and they'd grown up together, but it wasn't his business. He barely knew Gabriel, and he had nothing to say about it.

"I'm not well-off either, not anymore. And Alice is right. I know a lot of people would do pretty much anything to go to college on someone else's dime. I never wanted to go, though. Why should I waste years of my life on something I'll hate? I'd rather do a job I like and start earning money. I already do. I've been working as a mechanic, which is how I put away enough money to leave home."

Alice shook her head. "Maybe."

Cyn was pretty sure nothing he could say would convince her she was wrong. Still, he added, "Besides, doing what my parents want wouldn't stop with college. They've already picked a wife for me, and since I didn't want to go to college, they expect me to marry her in the next few months."

Gabriel blinked. "They *picked* you a wife?"

"Yes. I think she's the daughter of a friend of a friend of my mother's or something like that. Anyway, I'm sure she's a nice girl and all, but I've never met her, and I'm not about to marry her. I wouldn't even if she were my type, and she's not."

"How do you know that?" Alice asked. She seemed bent on finding something wrong with every single decision Cyn made, didn't she?

"Because I'm gay, Alice. It wouldn't be fair to the girl or to me. Besides, what would *you* do if your parents forced you to marry someone you didn't know because of money or the prestige it would bring to your family?"

Alice's expression hardened. "I ran away when I was thirteen because my stepfather tried to sneak into my bed, and when I told my mother, she accused me of trying to seduce him. I doubt either of them would have tried to arrange a marriage for me, but if they had, I'd probably have gone through with it."

She turned around and disappeared back into the room where she'd come from. Cyn wasn't sure what to think of her or her story. He didn't doubt her sincerity, and he was sorry for what had happened to her, but he didn't see how it related to him and his presence here.

"I'm sorry," Gabriel murmured.

Cyn shook himself. Whatever Alice's problem was, whatever she thought of him, he wasn't there for her. "It's okay. It's obvious she's still hurting over it, and I get it, even though I didn't go through anything that hard. For what it's worth, I'm sorry for what happened to her." He doubted it was worth much to Alice, but it was all he could offer.

"I'll be sure to tell her. Why don't we go for that walk? Alice is studying, so she can probably use some peace."

"Let's go." Cyn was over the moon at being able to leave Alice behind. He had nothing against her, but it was obvious she didn't like him, even though they'd only talked for a minute. Cyn didn't care much, but it might make Gabriel's life hard, and he didn't want that to happen. He didn't want Gabriel to have to choose between his best friend since they were teenagers and a guy he'd met the day before. Who he'd choose was obvious, and Cyn didn't want to risk it. He wasn't going to let Alice badmouth him when he was right there in front of her, but there wasn't much he could do for when he wasn't there. He hoped Gabriel would like him enough by the end of the day to try to find out who Cyn was rather than listen to what Alice had to say.

He wouldn't bet on it, though.

Gabriel had no idea what had happened. He'd hoped Alice

and Cyn would get along, or at least that they'd be okay with each other, but for some reason, Alice had decided to attack Cyn over things that, though they made sense, weren't her business.

Gabriel understood why she was bewildered that Cyn had left home because his parents wanted him to go to college. Things had sounded more serious than that from the rest Cyn had said, but Gabriel knew Alice had stopped listening when she'd heard that Cyn didn't want to go to college. To her and Gabriel, college represented a goal, something they couldn't have had if they hadn't pulled themselves off the streets thirteen years ago. They'd had help, of course, but graduating from college was something they'd wanted to do on their own, a way to show they *could* do it.

It didn't represent the same thing for Cyn, though, and that was okay. Alice would eventually realize it.

She had to.

Gabriel wanted his mate and his best friend to get along. He wanted both of them in his life, and that wasn't going to work if they were at each other's throats. He understood why Alice had been so defensive, but he hoped she'd relax the next time she saw Cyn. Gabriel didn't want to have to choose between them. He wouldn't be able to, even if they asked him to. It would be like asking him to choose between his eyes or his arms or something.

"Where are you taking me?" Cyn asked as he bounced down the porch steps. Gabriel didn't remember ever having that much energy, even at nineteen. Just watching Cyn bounce around made him tired, which was possibly a sign that he was turning into an old man before his time.

Still, it made him smile. Maybe he *needed* that kind of energy in his life. "I didn't have a destination in mind. I suppose I should show you the main areas, like where the infirmary is, the fire pit, things like that. That way you can orient yourself even on your own. And you should probably visit Kameron and Zach. They're the alpha and the alpha mate, and while they don't mind visitors, they'll need to know if you're going to stick around."

"I've never been part of a pack. Most days, I feel like I've never been part of a family."

"Do you want to talk about it?" Gabriel knew he was delaying the inevitable—he was going to tell Cyn they were mates while they were alone in the forest because it was the right thing to do, even though it wasn't the easiest one.

Cyn shrugged and pushed his hands into the pockets of his jeans. "I already told you the important bits. There's not much love between my parents and me. Never has been. They had me because it was expected of them. That's what marriages are for, you know? Their parents arranged everything, and they never fell in love. Some days I wonder if they even tolerate each other, because it seems that the only times they talk and get along is when they berate me for something or other."

Gabriel couldn't wrap his mind around arranged marriages, maybe because he'd seen so much love ever since he'd arrived in Gillham. There were a lot of bonded couples here, and while their lives weren't always flowers and butterflies, they loved each other, and it was evident to everyone. Even his own parents had loved each other. They hadn't loved *him* enough to keep him when they'd found out the baby they'd adopted was a shifter, and gay to boot.

"You don't need to look so sad for me," Cyn gently teased.

"I'm sorry. I was thinking about how, well, sad it is."

"I know I grew up privileged, trust me. I had a roof over my head and everything I could ask for. Food, money, clothes, whatever. My life was easier than yours or Alice's."

"I understand where Alice was coming from, but that doesn't mean I share her views, or that you have to apologize to me for the way you've lived until now. You didn't have a choice in the family you were born in, just like Alice and I didn't. You're trying to make your own decisions and live your life the way you want it, and you're ready to give up a lot to do that. It's impressive." Especially at nineteen. Gabriel and Alice had already been alone several years by the time they reached that age, even counting the years they'd been with the foster family here in Gillham. Gabriel knew how hard it was to make your own way, and in a way, it had been easier for him. No one had expected anything from him, while Cyn's parents clearly had a lot of dreams, or rather, a lot of demands. "What did they want you to study?"

Cyn huffed. "Law. My father is an associate in a law firm. He wants me to follow in this footsteps and work with him after college."

"But you said you want to be a mechanic." Gabriel had a hard time imagining Cyn working on a car. He looked, well, kind of preppy, with his button-down shirt and nice jeans. That was only appearances, though, of course. Cyn was already revealing himself to be much more than Gabriel had thought or expected.

Cyn's expression brightened. "Yes. My parents would have a fit if they knew, of course. They never found out that their driver taught me to work on their cars. Once I was able to do stuff on my own, some of my friends from school came to me and asked me to look over their cars. It was risky, because my parents might have found out, but it helped me put money aside to leave. Between that and the money my grandparents left me, I should be able to get an apartment and maybe even look into opening my shop."

"You should try talking to Oliver."

Cyn cocked his head. His tail was moving with every step he took, and Gabriel was glad they were both walking because it would have been easy to lose himself in the sight. It was hypnotic, and he couldn't help but wonder what the tail felt like.

"Oliver?" Cyn asked.

"He's a mechanic, too, although his main focus is on bikes. He has a shop in town. He fixes them, of course, but he also personalizes them."

Cyn looked like Gabriel had offered him the moon. "Really? It would be cool to learn stuff from him. I've never worked on a bike. I wonder how different it is from a car, beyond the obvious, of course."

Gabriel chuckled. "I wouldn't know. I've always been more interested in books than in cars and bikes. I'd probably make the engine explode if you asked me to try to fix a car."

"You like books?"

"I'm a librarian. It's kind of a requisite when you do my job."

Cyn arched a brow and looked Gabriel up and down. "I can't say I would have thought you're a librarian."

"Because I don't have glasses or wear cardigans?"

Cyn laughed. "Maybe. I guess I'm biased by the dragon lady that handled the library when I was at school. She loved her books, and she made sure you paid if you ruined one. It wasn't a problem, considering everyone in that school was as rich as me, but yeah. She was scary."

"And I'm not?" Gabriel knew he wasn't, and he didn't want to be, but he was having a lot of fun bantering with Cyn.

"You're cute, adorable, all kinds of sexy, but not scary, no."

Gabriel's cheeks heated. It was ridiculous—he was twenty-nine, and he'd been flirted with plenty of times—but he couldn't help it.

"Did I overstep?" Cyn asked. "I don't want to create problems between you and Alice."

Gabriel frowned. "Me and Alice?"

"I know you said you were best friends, but I can't help but wonder if there's more. I know not everyone loves me, but she was especially harsh, and I have a hard time believing it's only about college. I mean, I know you two didn't have the same opportunities I've had, but that doesn't mean I should go to college even though I don't want to."

"We're not together. We've never been together, and it's never going to happen."

"No?"

There was a lot of hope in Cyn's expression, a hope he probably didn't fully understand. This felt like the perfect moment to tell him they were mates, but it was still petrifying, to the point that Gabriel was finding it hard to breathe.

He swallowed. "I'm gay, but even if I were bi, she's like a little sister to me, and there's my mate. I won't ever be with anyone else, not unless he tells me he doesn't want me."

Cyn's smile fell, and Gabriel realized he hadn't actually told him *he* was his mate.

"It's you," he blurted out.

Cyn blinked. "It's me, what?"

"My mate. It's you. You're my mate."

Cyn wasn't sure he'd heard that right. "What?" he croaked, needing the confirmation.

"I know I shouldn't have told you that way. I'm sorry. I wasn't sure how to say it. I doubt there's a right way to tell a stranger that they're your mate, and I'm aware of the fact that demons don't have mates in the first place. But I swear, I'm not lying."

Cyn had never thought he was. He'd needed to hear the words again because he wasn't sure he could trust his ears the first time, not when it came to something so important. "I'm your mate. You're sure?"

Gabriel gave a hard nod. "A hundred percent. This isn't something I'd joke about. I should probably have told you last night, but I was in shock, and—"

Cyn leaned forward and kissed Gabriel's cheek. He wasn't sure when they'd stopped walking or if Gabriel would be down with the kiss, but he wanted Gabriel to know this was okay, and he wasn't sure he could form the words. He was shocked, more so than he'd ever been, and he had no idea how to deal with that.

Gabriel blinked but didn't push Cyn away. "Does this mean you're okay with being my mate?"

"Yeah. I guess." Cyn rubbed the back of his neck. "I can't say I'm not surprised, because I didn't expect anything like this to happen, but I'll get used to it." He couldn't help but think that this would never have happened if he hadn't decided to stand up to his parents and leave home. The thought was horrifying, even though he and Gabriel didn't know each other yet. Cyn would have lost so much if he'd bowed to his parents and followed their orders. He'd have studied for years for a job he'd have hated. He would have married a woman he wouldn't have cared about. He wouldn't have met Gabriel, and even though their future was anything but set in stone, he wouldn't have had the opportunity to have the kind of bond he'd seen between his cousin and his mate last night.

His life right now made his head spin with the possibilities and the newness of it.

"Do you want to sit down? You look like you need it," Gabriel suggested.

Cyn looked around. He didn't care if he sat on the ground, but he didn't want Gabriel to have to. "Where's the nearest bench?"

Gabriel laughed. He wasn't as tense as he'd been before, and Cyn realized it must be because he'd confessed the mate thing. He'd probably been afraid Cyn wouldn't take it well. It wasn't something Cyn had ever thought of, not even in his wildest fantasies, in which he'd have a home and a shop and be happy with a new family. Like Gabriel had said, demons didn't have mates, and what were the chances that he was a shifter's mate and that he'd meet the man?

It seemed like those chances had been pretty high, actually, and the thought made Cyn chuckle.

"We're not far from the community center and the fire pit. There are benches there, or in the forest around it, if you're not up for company. At this time of the day, the moms are there with the kids, so it's fairly noisy."

Cyn didn't care, but for some reason, he doubted Gabriel wanted an audience. He had no idea what was going to happen—probably nothing more than a chat—but he wanted privacy to break down and behave like a happy idiot if he wanted to. "Let's go to one of those benches in the trees."

Gabriel led the way, and it gave Cyn a few minutes to start wrapping his mind around things.

He had a mate. He was *Gabriel's* mate, and that meant a lot. They'd be together forever once they bonded. They'd be each other's rock, the harbor against the storm, the home to come back to at night. It wasn't something Cyn had thought of or realized he'd wanted, but God, he did, so very much. He wanted all that with Gabriel, even though he barely knew him. That was the bond, right? Demons might not have mates, just like humans, but like humans, they could feel the draw to their mate, especially once they were aware of them. Cyn didn't mind that Gabriel had waited to tell him—it was only a day, and last night had been emotional enough for Cyn even without adding the mate thing to the situation. It was hard to imagine Gabriel knowing and keeping it to himself, though. Cyn wanted to shout it from the rooftops.

"Did Alice know?" he asked. He was going to tell Noah as soon as he could, if Gabriel was okay with it. He wanted to share his happiness, and he didn't have anyone else to do it with. He'd had a few friends in school, but none of them would want to know about this. None of them would care. They were all like Cyn's parents, which was why he wasn't regretting leaving them behind.

"I think that's one of the reasons she was the way she was earlier," Gabriel said. "I told her and Oliver, and while they were both happy, Alice was also a bit wary."

Cyn understood that, but he was also slightly offended. "She doesn't know me. I haven't done anything to make her think I'm not a good person."

"I know. But it's been only us for a long time, and she's never taken change well. We relied on each other and only each other for so long. I think that having you in my life is threatening that in her eyes, and in some ways, it does. She was the most important person for me until now. She'll still be important, but it won't be the same, and we'll both have to learn to deal with that, you know?"

"I see." Cyn did understand, but he also wished Alice would give him a chance. Maybe she would, eventually. He wanted to explore what he and Gabriel could have, but that wasn't going to happen if Alice despised him. He wasn't sure there was anything he could do to change that, though. He hadn't said anything to make her hate him, or at least he didn't think so. As far as he could see, the main reason she disliked him was that he didn't want to go to college even though he wouldn't have to pay a dime to do so while Gabriel was overworking himself to make sure she had that opportunity. As unfair as the situation was, there was nothing Cyn could do about it. He wasn't going to change his mind and go to college, not when merely thinking about it gave him hives. Books and whatnot weren't what he enjoyed, and no amount of disliking from anyone was going to change that.

"She's also very protective of me. She worries. Even though we had foster parents once we moved here, we've always been a unit. We cared for each other, took care of each other. She wants to be sure you're the best I can have."

"Isn't that kind of the point of mates? Being perfect for each other?"

"In theory, sure, but that doesn't mean it's a universal thing. Some mates aren't good people. But she'll soften, you'll see. She's my best friend, and she wants me to be happy."

Cyn wanted to believe that, but he was wary. Alice was overprotective, there was no denying that, and he was afraid that more than Gabriel himself, she wanted to protect what they had. Like Gabriel had said, they'd been a unit for more than a decade, and Cyn was throwing a wrench into that by existing. He had no idea what Gabriel was going to do if he had to choose. He wasn't going to give Gabriel an ultimatum, but Alice might, and that thought was terrifying.

It shouldn't be. Cyn had been without a mate until now. He hadn't planned on ever having one, or on finding himself a boyfriend so soon after leaving home. He didn't *need* Gabriel, but he wanted him and the promise of what having him in his life would bring.

He wanted to be happy and to choose how he lived his life. He would do that anyway, with or without Gabriel, but he'd rather do it with him than alone.

CHAPTER FOUR

Gabriel was happy. He was whistling as he chose the clothes from his closet, singing as he put them on after his shower. He hadn't been unhappy before, but he'd been so focused on working and earning money that he hadn't let himself think about anything else. Now that Cyn was in his life, though, he couldn't stop thinking about him.

They'd seen each other every day since they'd met the week before. They hadn't done anything serious, but this was more dating than Gabriel could ever remember doing. He'd had a few boyfriends over the years, but most of them hadn't been able to understand why he was so focused on studying and work and why he wanted to support Alice the way he did. He wasn't sure Cyn understood, either, but he hadn't said anything about it, and he didn't argue when Gabriel was late because of work, or when he had to leave early. He wasn't perfect, but he was as close to it as anyone could get.

He was still humming when he left the house on his way to work, holding his battered cup of coffee and his messenger bag.

He froze at the sight in front of him when he opened the door, and he had to blink to make sure he was seeing right.

A big vase full of flowers had been left on the welcome mat. There was a note, and Gabriel gently plucked it to make sure the flowers were for him and not for Alice or their next-door neighbor.

They weren't. They were for Gabriel, as was the new travel coffee cup in the bag next to the flowers.

"What's that?" Alice asked from behind Gabriel. She sounded sleepy, but she straightened as soon as Gabriel stepped aside to show her. "The fuck?"

Gabriel prayed he wasn't going to be late and picked up the flowers. Alice took care of the bag with the mug, and they headed to the kitchen. Gabriel checked that there was water in the vase, and thank God, there was, so he wouldn't have to worry about that.

"Are those for *you*?" Alice asked.

"You don't have to sound so surprised." It was a bit hurtful, as if she couldn't believe someone would think of Gabriel and send him flowers to let him know that.

"Flowers are a waste of money."

"And now you sound jealous." Gabriel didn't want to fight with Alice, especially not right now, because it would make him late for work. Besides, she *was* a bit bitchy, and Gabriel had done nothing to warrant that. Neither had Cyn, whom the flowers were from, and Gabriel was starting to get annoyed with the way Alice was treating him.

"I'm not jealous." Alice huffed and crossed her arms over her chest. "But this guy left home, right? He said that his parents aren't going to pay his way anymore, yet he buys you those flowers? They're expensive, Gabe."

Gabriel had suspected that. "So? I'm sure he has the means to afford them. He's been putting away money for years, and his grandparents created a fund for him when he was a kid. That's his, not his parents'."

"So he's still not living on his own two feet. It's still someone else paying for him."

Gabriel grunted. He was going to be late. He shouldn't engage now, especially not with how angry Alice was. "It's not his fault that he was luckier than us. You shouldn't use that against him, just like no one should use the fact that we lived on the streets against us. I understand you're angry and scared, Alice, but that doesn't give you the right to treat Cyn like shit. He hasn't done anything to you, and he's been a perfect gentleman to me. You're hurting me, and I don't like it. Now if you'll excuse me, I'm already late as it is."

Gabriel turned and left the kitchen, ignoring Alice's calls for him to wait. He couldn't wait. He didn't *want* to wait. He wanted to go to work and lose himself in his books, not think about how complicated his life had gotten and how his feelings were a mix of giddiness and irritation.

It had somewhat faded by the time he got to the library. Being there always soothed him, maybe because he'd lost himself in books to forget about real life when he was a teenager. He was still annoyed by Alice's reaction, but he forced himself to ignore that and to focus on the flowers and the mug.

They were thoughtful gifts. No one had ever given Gabriel flowers, and he'd always thought it would be a waste anyway, since the flowers eventually died. He was touched, though, both by the flowers and by the mug, but especially by the mug. Gabriel wasn't sure how or when, but Cyn had noticed he needed a new one, and that was worth more than any amount of money Cyn had spent. It meant he was getting to know Gabriel and that he noticed little things Gabriel wasn't telling him about. He was interested in Gabriel, and Gabriel was interested in him.

He needed to focus on his work so he could call Cyn and thank him during his lunch break.

Gabriel started working, holding the warmth of Cyn's gifts close to his chest as he did so. It would be too easy to focus on the bad stuff. He usually did. He didn't want to this time around, though.

"You look awfully chipper," Oliver said when he leaned over the counter at the entrance of the library.

Gabriel was sitting there now that he'd finished putting the books back on the shelves.

Gabriel grinned at him. "Why wouldn't I be?"

"Right. Alice told me about the flowers."

Gabriel sighed and leaned back in his chair. "Let me guess. She also told you how awful Cyn is because he can afford to spend that money on something as stupid as flowers."

Oliver grimaced. "That's not precisely how she put it, but yeah, pretty much. She sure seems to have a grudge against him."

"She does, and I have no idea why."

"Yeah, you do. She told me about him, you know. She called me the day after she met him, and she keeps texting me to complain. She has it out for him. She's jealous."

"I didn't expect this to happen."

"Because you didn't expect to meet your mate. But you and Alice have been together for a long time, and she sees Cyn as intruding on that. Add to it the fact that he comes from money and that he decided to say fuck you to that because he didn't want to go to college, and she's pissed."

"That's what she told you? That he left home because he didn't want to go to college?"

"And that his grandparents were still passing him money."

Gabriel didn't know if Alice had lied or if she hadn't understood what Gabriel had told her this morning. He wasn't sure it mattered. "His grandparents aren't giving him anything. They set up a trust fund when he was born, and he's using that money and the money he earned as a mechanic right now. He's looking for an apartment, and for a job."

Oliver's eyes lit up. "A mechanic?"

"Yeah. I was supposed to tell you about it, but I forgot. He's focused on cars, so I don't know if you're interested in that."

"Oh, I am. I can't wait to have a chat with him. You said he's looking for a job?"

"He is. He hasn't found anything yet as far as I know, but

he's not a freeloader, and he's not waiting for other people to do this stuff for him. And he didn't leave home because he didn't want to go to college, at least not entirely."

Oliver raised his hands. "I was telling you what Alice said. I don't know your mate since I haven't seen him except for that first night, but he's your mate. He can't be a bad person."

Bad, no, but Gabriel couldn't deny Cyn was a bit naïve and that he expected life to be easy. It *wasn't* a bad thing, but it was one more thing that grated on Alice's nerves. "He's not."

"And I suggest you and Alice sit down for a chat. Whatever her problem is, Cyn isn't going anywhere, since you seem to want him in your life, and Alice needs to get used to that idea."

Gabriel wasn't sure she ever would, and the thought made his stomach churn.

Cyn wasn't bouncing on his feet, but he might as well be. He didn't think he'd ever been this happy in his life, although he supposed that at nineteen, he hadn't lived long, either. Still, the thought of seeing Gabriel made his stomach churn in a pleasant way, and he was looking forward to it. He hoped Gabriel had liked the flowers and the cup. He'd noticed Gabriel's travel mug was old and had probably fallen more than once, and he'd thought it would be a nice *thinking-of-you* present.

Life was good and certainly better than it had been for Cyn growing up. He'd been in Gillham a week, and in that time, he'd met his mate, had officially become a pack member after talking to Kameron and Zach, and he was looking for an apartment. He got along great with Noah, even though Noah was much older, and Noah had told him he didn't have to rush to move out. Cyn was tempted to hang around, because he wasn't used to being on his own, but it was time. He was an adult, and he'd left home to live his life. He needed to start.

He climbed the porch steps to Gabriel's front door and gave a quick knock. He knew Gabriel had work today, of course, but he'd hinted at possibly coming home for lunch since he worked in town and his daily commute was five minutes long, ten at the most. Cyn hadn't heard from him, and they hadn't planned to meet, but if Gabriel had managed to get home, Cyn wanted to surprise him. If he was stuck at work, well, maybe Cyn would call and see if he wanted to grab a quick sandwich.

He knocked and waited, holding his breath when he heard footsteps on the other side. He stood straighter and started to smile, but the smile quickly faded when the door opened, and Alice was revealed. She looked Cyn up and down, and he wondered if that was a look of disgust on her face. It *definitely* was annoyance, even though he hadn't done anything to warrant that.

"What do you want?" Alice asked. She sounded like Cyn was interrupting her, and he probably was. He knew she was studying for her exams or something like that. He hadn't asked for details because he found the whole college thing boring and complicated—which was one of the reasons he didn't want to go.

"Is Gabriel home?"

Alice arched a brow. "You really *are* disconnected from what real people's lives are, aren't you?"

What the fuck? "I'm sorry?"

"Gabriel is at work. You know, that place where people go every day because they need to earn money to survive? Gabriel has bills to pay, you know. He can't afford to stay at home and take advantage of other people's kindness."

"You mean the way you are taking advantage of his?" Cyn snapped. He regretted the words as soon as they were out of his mouth. He didn't want to fight with Alice, no matter how nasty she was with him. She was Gabriel's best friend, and while Cyn didn't understand why they were so close and why she was behaving like this, he didn't want Gabriel to have to choose between them. That would happen if they fought.

Her cheeks reddened. "How dare you—"

Cyn raised his hands. "I'm sorry. I didn't mean to snap. But I don't understand what I did to you. I know you hate the fact that I didn't go to college, but I don't see how that matters to you. I made the choice I thought was right for my life, just like you did, no matter the sacrifices you have to make." And the sacrifices *Gabriel* had to make, but Cyn doubted Alice would be happy to be reminded of that, so he didn't add it.

Alice scoffed. "Sacrifices? What do you know about that? Having to leave behind your expensive car and luxury clothes isn't a sacrifice, especially when you didn't *have* to do it."

"I know that when you left home—"

"You know nothing of my life and what happened to me, so don't you *dare* say anything about it."

Cyn snapped his mouth shut. It was true he didn't know much about Alice, and right now, he didn't want to find out. Whatever had happened to her in the past didn't mean she could be rude, and it didn't give her a reason to hate him as much as she seemed to. He hadn't done anything to her. He'd been lucky to be born into a family with money while she'd been born into a family that ultimately had pushed her out, but what could Cyn do about that? He'd already distanced himself from his parents. He'd left most of the stuff he'd bought with their money behind. He'd left the car his father had bought for him, and like Alice had said, his luxury clothes. He didn't need them anyway, not when he was planning on spending a lot of time under cars and rolling around in grease.

What more did Alice want from him?

Cyn cleared his throat. "Gabriel mentioned he might come home for lunch. That's all."

Alice's expression tightened. "He has to work, but again, what do you know about that? Have you found a job since you got here?"

"Not yet." He'd interviewed with Andy, the man who owned the mechanic shop in town. Cyn wasn't stupid enough to try to start his own shop when he had no real experience. He'd worked on a lot of cars, and he knew what he was doing, but from there to being a business owner, it would take time. He needed to learn, and he was more than ready to do that.

"Not yet. Of course."

Cyn pressed his lips together. "What have I done to you? I can't help the family I was born into any more than you can. I'm trying to find my way in life, and yes, I refused to go to college and gave up a lot of money coming here, whatever you seem to think of it. I'm not asking you to like me, but I'd appreciate it if you were at least civil to me since I'm your best friend's mate."

"You might be Gabriel's mate, but you're nowhere good enough for him." She narrowed her eyes and leaned closer. "You're a spoiled rich kid who doesn't think twice about buying expensive flowers when that money could have been used for grocery shopping. And what have you ever done that wasn't for yourself? Gabriel never thinks about himself. He's too selfless for that. He's always doing everything he can to help others, and you're his exact opposite."

There was a hint of truth in there. It *was* true that all of Cyn's decisions until now had been done for himself. He'd said no to college for himself. He'd left home for himself. Was that such a bad thing, though? He didn't think so, but Alice did. "I don't think I can help people before I help myself."

Alice snorted. "Bullshit. You're settling down in another luxurious life. It might not be as good as the one you left behind only because you didn't want to go to college, but it's still nowhere as hard as Gabriel and my lives were or are. You have enough money to be able to afford not to work for more than a week. You have a family, and you get to be with them. You have no idea how the world works for people like us. You're a spoiled kid, and Gabriel deserves so much better than you."

She stepped back and slammed the door in Cyn's face. He blinked at it and wondered what the fuck had just happened.

Some of Alice's words had hit home, though. She wasn't wrong when she'd said that Cyn was spoiled. He'd never know what being hungry was like. He'd never known what not having someone to rely on was like. He might not have grown up with love, but that didn't change the fact that he'd been incredibly lucky, and what was he doing to repay that?

He needed to find a job and an apartment, but he felt like that wasn't going to be enough. He needed to be worthy of Gabriel, to show him he could be a good mate and a good person.

How was he supposed to do that, though?

Cyn hadn't texted today. He also hadn't called, and Gabriel was worried.

He knew it was probably ridiculous—Cyn was busy trying to find an apartment and a job, and he'd shown he was thinking about Gabriel when he'd left the flowers and the mug on the porch that morning. Gabriel wished he'd had time to go home for lunch to see Cyn, or at least to call him, but he'd been too busy to eat anything more than a sandwich at his desk. And once his work at the library was done, he'd had to rush over to the shelter. He hadn't been putting as many hours there as he usually did because he tried to spend at least an hour with Cyn every day, and that meant he had to cram the same amount of work as before in less time, which wasn't an easy thing to do. But then nothing in his life was easy, or at least, nothing had been until he met Cyn.

His relationship with Cyn *felt* easy. Cyn wasn't a worrier. He didn't have a job yet, or an apartment, but he had the means to go on even without those, at least for a while. He wanted to do things the right way, even if it meant waiting. Gabriel wished he could do the same, but he didn't have that luxury, not when every penny he earned went to repay his debt to the pack and college for Alice. They didn't pay rent — and Gabriel had allowed that only because none of the other pack members did — but there were utilities and groceries to pay for, too, and that didn't leave anything in his bank account by the end of the month.

But Cyn had the luxury to take his time, and that wasn't a bad thing. He wouldn't make mistakes if he could think things out.

Gabriel had missed him today, so instead of driving straight home like he usually did, he headed toward Noah and Duncan's home. He'd never been there, even though he knew where it was, and he hoped he wouldn't disturb them. He should probably have called Cyn before going, but Cyn wasn't answering his texts, and Gabriel was getting worried, which was probably ridiculous. Why should he be worried? It wasn't like he and Cyn needed to be attached at the hip. Cyn had his stuff to do, even though he wasn't working, and Gabriel wasn't so insecure that he needed to spend all his free time with his mate. However, they were still getting to know each other, and not knowing what was going on made Gabriel uneasy.

He climbed out of the car when he got to Noah's house and made a beeline for the door before he could think better of it and head home. He knocked, and from what Cyn had told him, he wasn't surprised when Duncan was the one who answered. Duncan smiled at him and stepped aside to let him in before he even told him why he was there.

"Cyn is in his room," Duncan said.

"Do you know if something has happened?" Gabriel probably shouldn't ask Duncan that, but he wanted to be warned if there *was* a problem.

"Honestly? I'm not sure. I don't know Cyn that well, but in the week he's been here, he's been smiling and talking most of the time. He was fine this morning, but when he came back after lunch, he was a bit down. Noah and I didn't ask, but I can't say I'm sorry you're here. We have no idea how to deal with a moody teenager."

Gabriel's cheeks flushed. "He's not a teenager anymore."

"Right. Sorry. What I meant is that we don't know him well enough to ask him what's wrong, and while you've known him as long as I have, you're in a better place to do that. Feel free to stay the night if you need to, and don't bother looking for us to say goodbye. Noah is in his studio painting, and I have some work to do." Duncan smiled and patted Gabriel's shoulder. "I'm looking forward to getting to know you when things get easier."

Now Gabriel was scared. "Same."

Duncan explained where Cyn's room was, and Gabriel climbed the stairs. The house was cozy, and there were colorful paintings on nearly every wall he passed. He was nervous when he knocked on the door of Cyn's bedroom, but even more so when the door opened, and he could tell right away that something *was* wrong.

"What happened?" he asked Cyn.

Cyn frowned. "Nothing. What are you doing here? Did we decide to meet?"

"No. I was worried about you." Gabriel shuffled. "Thank you for the flowers. I didn't expect them, and they were a very nice start to my day."

Cyn nodded. "I'm glad you liked them, even though I realize I should probably have done something more constructive with that money."

Gabriel blinked. Where had that come from? Cyn had been liberal with his money until now, offering Gabriel dinner several times. Gabriel wasn't offended by it. Cyn had more money than he did, but that didn't mean anything. It was Cyn's, and he could do whatever he wanted with it. Gabriel had no reason to resent him, and he didn't. "I liked them. No one has ever bought me flowers before. Cyn, why are you saying that it was a waste of money?"

"I didn't say that."

"Not in those words, no."

Cyn sighed. "Look, Gabriel, I'm worried, okay? I haven't found a place yet, and I don't have a job. I'm living off the money my grandparents earned, and that's not right."

Gabriel narrowed his eyes. "I told you I might go home for lunch today."

"Yeah, you did."

"Did you go there? Did you want to have lunch with me?"

Cyn looked down and shuffled. "Yeah."

"And Alice was home."

Cyn nodded. "She was. But she didn't say anything that wasn't true."

Gabriel shook his head. He had a pretty good idea of what Alice had said, and he was going to kick her ass as soon as he got home. Not literally, of course, but she had no right to do this. She had no right to stick her nose into their relationship. Gabriel could make his own decisions, and he'd decided he wanted to be with Cyn. He didn't care about the money or the fact that while Cyn had plans, he still was a little lost.

He reached for Cyn, cupping both his cheeks and enjoying the way Cyn's eyes went round. He leaned forward and pressed their lips together, and to his relief, Cyn leaned closer, kissing him back. It wasn't a solution, but it helped for a moment, and Gabriel felt better. Whatever Alice had told Cyn, he wasn't giving up on them. He might be hurt and battered, but Gabriel could solve this. He was going to make sure of that.

"You owe no one anything," he said against Cyn's lips.

Cyn moved back. "I know."

"I'm not sure you do. You weren't responsible for what happened to Alice and me. What we had to go through was hard and unfair, but you had nothing to do with it, and she shouldn't pin that on you. She also shouldn't dislike you for your parents and how much money they have. I know that telling you to ignore her isn't going to help and that she's already hurt you, but none of what she said matters to me, okay?"

Cyn finally smiled. "You don't know what she said."

"Not for sure, but I can imagine, and I'm not happy. It's not fair to you, and even if it was, she shouldn't tell you any of that. Being with you is a decision *I* need to make, and I don't need her to try to push you away for an imagined slight."

"I don't want you to fight with her. She's your best friend."

"Then she should act like it, and being mean to you when you're not doing anything wrong isn't the way to do that."

"She's worried about you. She doesn't want you to get hurt."

"And I won't, but even if you *do* hurt me, it'll be your and my business, not hers. She can talk to me if she's worried, but she shouldn't attack you." Especially not when Cyn had only been trying to be a sweet mate and to make Gabriel happy. Gabriel had been so focused on work until now that the flowers had made his day.

Someone was thinking about him. *Cyn* was thinking about him, and he wanted to make him happy. Gabriel wasn't going to let anyone ruin that, not even Alice.

Cyn watched Gabriel leave. He kind of wanted to be a fly on

the wall of the conversation his mate was about to have with his best friend, but he knew that his presence there would make things explosive and worse than they already were. Alice would hate it if he was there, and she'd get defensive. No matter what she'd said, Cyn still didn't want Gabriel and Alice to fight. They needed to talk and clear things up, but Cyn hoped they could find a way out of this.

Maybe admitting that Alice was partially right was the first step in that direction for him.

He hated the thought, but it *was* true that he was living on his grandparents' money right now. He had some money saved that he'd earned, but it wouldn't be enough for him to survive for long. He had to get a move on and start settling his life, which was what he'd been planning to do all along. He'd gotten himself lost in meeting Gabriel and his newfound relationship with Noah, though.

It was time to grow up.

"Cyn?" Noah called from the hallway.

"Come in."

Cyn didn't get up from the bed, and Noah flopped next to him on the mattress, face up and hair dirty with paint. "Are you going to tell me what happened?"

Cyn groaned. "I don't want to." He didn't want to talk about it, and he wanted to stop thinking about it, too.

"I'm not going to push."

"But you're going to stay here until I tell you, right?"

Noah grinned. "Pretty much. I'm glad you seem to know me so well already."

Cyn sighed. "I went to see Gabriel earlier, but he wasn't home. Alice was, though."

Noah grimaced.

Cyn had told him and Duncan about the fact that Alice seemed to hate him, so they knew part of the situation.

"She wasn't happy to see you, I take it."

"Not even a little bit. She tore into me for buying Gabriel flowers when I could have used that money for grocery shopping. She told me I'm a spoiled brat that has no idea what sacrifice is or means and that I'm not worthy of Gabriel."

Noah whistled. "Damn. She didn't go easy on you."

"I know."

"You also know she's not right, don't you? Because while it might be true that you were spoiled, it doesn't make you a bad person. I was like you when I left home. I had no idea what I was doing. I'd never paid rent or gone to the grocery store. That doesn't mean I was a bad person. Privileged, yes, but not bad. As long as you're aware of that and that you learn to live a good life, I don't think it's a bad thing, and I'm sorry Alice seems so bent on hating you for something you had no control over."

Gabriel had already told Cyn all of that, but it felt good to hear it from someone else, even though that someone was his cousin. "I want to get better."

Noah arched a brow. "For Gabriel?"

"For him, and myself. He deserves a good mate, and I need to start living like everyone else."

"You need to live like you want to live, not like everyone else. Isn't that why you left home? Because you wanted to make your own way and rules?"

"Yeah."

"Then do it. What do you want to do?"

"I want to give back to people. I want to find a job and an apartment, even though I know you don't mind me staying here."

"You're right, I don't. I like having you here. We have a lot of catching up to do. But we can do it even if you live in town. I'm not going anywhere, and neither are you from now on. We're a family."

Cyn had known Noah felt that way, but it still felt good to

hear it. "We are."

"Okay. What's your next step, then? We can look at apartments together. Actually, we should call Kam and ask him what the pack has in town."

"I can pay for rent."

"I know you can, but I don't see why you should have to. Alice certainly isn't paying rent. Duncan and I aren't, either. The house here and some of the apartments in town belong to the pack. It's a way for Kam to take care of us. That way, no one has to be afraid they'll be out on the streets. You're not different, even though you have money."

"I—"

"Next stop is a job, yeah?"

Noah was going to steamroll Cyn, wasn't he? And he wasn't wrong. If no one in the pack paid for their housing, why should Cyn? He was officially a pack member. He'd talked with Kameron and Zach, answered a few questions, and they'd welcomed him with open arms and an offer to help for whatever he might need.

"I haven't heard back from Andy yet."

"What about Oliver? Or are you only interested in cars?"

Cyn frowned. "What about Oliver?" He hadn't seen Gabriel's friend again, and they hadn't talked about him much because, well, they'd been getting to know each other and talking about that.

"You know, Gabriel's friend? He has a shop. He works on motorcycles, though, and I have no idea how different that is from cars or if it's something you might be interested in. Maybe you could talk to him and Gabriel? See if Oliver needs someone."

"Wouldn't he hire me only because I'm Gabriel's mate?"

"Not if you suck. He'll give you more leeway because of it, sure, but people come to his shop from all around Gillham because of his reputation. He wouldn't risk ruining it by hiring someone who can't do the job, but I bet he'd be willing to teach you what you don't know. I mean, he didn't start knowing everything. Surely he'll want an apprentice."

"I don't know." But Cyn was interested. He'd only ever worked on cars because that was what his parents and his friends drove. Working on motorcycles sounded good, though, like a challenge he wanted to pick up.

Noah patted Cyn's thigh. "Just think about it and contact both Oliver and Kam. See what they say. You might have the physical means to start a new life on your own, but that doesn't mean you should. You're not alone, Cyn, no matter what you think or what your parents have told you."

"Thank you." Noah had given Cyn things to think about, that was for sure.

"Have they called?"

"My parents?"

"Yes."

"No. Have yours?"

Noah grinned. "My dad calls every week. He's the one to do it because I always forget."

It was nice that Noah had his father, but Cyn didn't resent him for that. He'd always known that his own father wouldn't want anything to do with him if he defied him, and that was how things had gone. Nothing was going to change, either.

"Oh, and if you want to give back to the community or whatever, you could always volunteer at the shelter where Gabriel works at night."

Cyn blinked. "What?" How had Noah gone from talking about his father to that?

"You know. He works at the shelter. No matter how hard Kameron and the mayor work, some people need help. That's what the shelter is for. Volunteers usually stick to helping with the meals, but Gabriel might be able to find something else for you to do."

"I don't want my whole life to revolve around him. My apartment, my job, and this, too."

Noah rolled his eyes. "I don't see what the problem is, but okay. Go to Gabriel's boss, then. She's always looking for more people. She'll find you something to do."

That was something Cyn hadn't thought about. Maybe Noah was right, and it would be a good way to give back. He'd been lucky in life—there were no two ways about it. He couldn't help all the people who hadn't been, but maybe he could do something for a few of them. It wouldn't be much, but it would be better than not doing anything, right? And if he went straight to Gabriel's boss, Gabriel wouldn't even have to know about it.

Cyn wasn't doing this for his mate—he was doing it for himself. He wanted to feel worthy of Gabriel and give back, to help people. He doubted anything he could do would help Alice soften toward him, but that wasn't going to stop him.

CHAPTER FIVE

For the first time in forever, Gabriel wished he could skip work at the shelter.

Wait, maybe that wasn't true. He usually wished he could because he was always so tired when it was time to go there, but today, Gabriel felt it more strongly. He didn't want to go to his second job. He wanted to spend time with his mate, to call Cyn and to see where he was, maybe to have dinner with him, to talk about their lives and their future.

But instead, Gabriel was heading to the shelter because he needed the money for Alice, to pay for college.

He wasn't rethinking that. Alice was his family, and nothing was going to change that. He wanted to make sure she wouldn't start life with debts and that she could do whatever she wanted. He hadn't minded doing it before because, being honest with himself, he didn't have a life, not outside his jobs. Now he did, though, and he was starting to realize that balancing two jobs and a mate wasn't going to be easy. He couldn't see a way out of it yet, but he was going to have to find one. He wasn't about to renounce Cyn's presence in his life, and he knew he'd be pushing Cyn away if he continued not having time for him. Cyn was understanding, but that could only go on for so long before he wanted more time with Gabriel and Gabriel couldn't give it to him.

Gabriel sighed and got out of his car after parking it in the back of the shelter. Now wasn't the time to think about this. He needed to focus on the job. Once that was done, he'd call Cyn, and they'd talk for a while, then Gabriel would go to bed and try to find a solution that might work.

He knew there was one. There had to be.

He locked his car and walked to the back door. It opened, almost hitting him in the face, and he glared at Oliver, who was dragging out two trash bags. "Watch it, Olivier."

Oliver glared at him. "I'm so sorry, *boss*. I'll check you're not hiding behind me the next time I have to throw the trash away."

"I wasn't hiding. I just got here."

"Main job ran late?"

"We had a meeting."

"Your man is already here."

Gabriel frowned. "My man?"

"Yeah. Your mate. I haven't had the chance to talk to him yet, though. Luke took care of showing him the ropes." Oliver chuckled. "I thought Cyn was going to run out. You know how intense Luke can sometimes be."

"Ollie, I have no idea what you're talking about."

"Well, Luke can be—"

"Not about that. Why is Cyn here?"

Oliver blinked as he cleaned his hands on his jeans. "You don't know?

"I wouldn't be asking if I did, and you better not touch me before you wash your hands."

"I will. He came to volunteer. I thought he'd talked to you about it, considering you're the guy in charge here and what-not."

"He never mentioned it." Was there a reason for him not to? Gabriel couldn't think of one, but he couldn't deny that Cyn had seemed to take a step back from whatever was growing between them lately. Gabriel had no idea what to do about it, though. He'd told Cyn that he didn't think the way Alice did. He'd hoped it would be enough, but maybe not. Maybe Cyn needed time. If he was there, willing to work with

Gabriel, that meant he wanted things to work out between them, right? If he didn't, he'd probably avoid Gabriel, and he hadn't been, even though he also hadn't been as forthcoming as he'd been before. He didn't call or text as often, but he answered every one of Gabriel's calls and texts.

"You two need to talk," Oliver said. "I wouldn't want to offer him a job only to have the two of you break up."

"We're not breaking up." Gabriel headed toward his office, Oliver trailing behind him. "We're learning to work things out.

"I can ask him to show me what he can do, then?"

"Of course. He told me he's mostly worked on cars, but he's interested in learning about bikes if you're willing to give him a chance."

Oliver grinned. "I am. And you *do* need to talk to him. I don't like the fact that he didn't tell you about this."

"Maybe he wanted it to be a surprise."

Oliver snorted. "A surprise? *Hey, love, look, I'm volunteering at the shelter where you work.* What kind of surprise is that?"

Gabriel ignored Oliver. He couldn't deny that this bugged him, but he didn't want to make it bigger than it probably was. Cyn was his mate, but that didn't mean they lived in each other's pockets, or that they had to tell each other everything. Cyn knew Gabriel worked there, and he probably hadn't thought to tell him he was going to volunteer. That was all.

Oliver sighed. "All right, I'll butt out of your business. But you should talk to him, Gabe."

"You already said that, and more than once. I'll talk to Cyn, don't worry. Don't you have things to do?"

Oliver grinned. "Yep. I'm going to take a wild guess that you and Cyn will leave together later, so I'll go ahead and go home."

"You do that." Gabriel's chest squeezed with the

knowledge that even though he'd been a bad friend for the past couple years, Oliver was still there, caring about him and making sure he was okay. He needed to find a way to earn as much money while working less. Gabriel missed his friends, and he wanted to spend more time with them.

He leaned against Oliver's side and kissed his cheek. Oliver blinked. "What was that for?" he asked.

Gabriel shrugged. "A thank you."

"What for?"

"Everything, I guess. Not giving up on me even though I'm not a great friend."

"That's not true. Even though we don't spend as much time together as I wish we did, I know why it's happening. You care, and you want everyone's lives to be perfect." Oliver hesitated. "Even though things don't work that way."

"Not perfect. Just, easier than mine has been."

Oliver nodded and patted Gabriel's shoulder as he left.

Gabriel knew talking about it again was a moot point, although maybe he was wrong this time. He wasn't as convinced as he'd been before. He did want to continue paying for Alice's college, but he wasn't sure he could go on like he had before.

But now wasn't the time to think about it. Gabriel left his office and went to look for Cyn. Oliver wasn't wrong when he'd said Cyn looked like he might run away. When Gabriel found him, his expression was bewildered as Luke gestured to the food they needed to serve tonight and the small bags containing deodorant and other toiletries. When he looked up and noticed Gabriel there, he yanked the net off his hair and fluffed it.

Gabriel smiled. Cyn's behavior was endearing, and it made Gabriel realize that in spite of the distance between them, Cyn wanted him in his life. He wouldn't be worried about the way he looked otherwise.

Gabriel waved Cyn closer, and after leaning closer to Luke and saying something to him, Cyn came. He shuffled in front of Gabriel like a kid caught with his hand in the cookie jar, and Gabriel knew he probably shouldn't find that adorable. "I didn't know you were planning to volunteer here," he said, unsure how to start this conversation.

Cyn shrugged. "I thought it was time for me to stop behaving like a spoiled brat and do something good with my life."

Gabriel frowned. That didn't sound like something Cyn would think of himself, and it wasn't true. Cyn might not know the world outside his demon town very well, and he might be used to having anything he wanted, but that didn't make him a bad person. No matter how spoiled he'd been materially, emotionally, he'd been left aside, and that was something Gabriel wanted to help him heal from. "You're not a spoiled brat."

"You can't deny I've had everything I wanted in my life."

Except for love. "Who told you you were a spoiled brat?"

Cyn avoided looking Gabriel in the eyes. "No one."

"Alice." If she hadn't said those exact words, she'd gone close enough to push Cyn to volunteer at the shelter. The volunteering part wasn't a bad thing, but Gabriel was angry with her. No matter what she was to Gabriel, she had no right to say anything like that to Cyn.

Gabriel quickly looked around, then took Cyn's hand and kissed him. "You are *not* a spoiled brat. Don't listen to Alice. I don't know what her problem is, but I'll talk to her, and she has nothing to say about our relationship. We're the only two people involved, and I hope what I think of you means more to you than what she thinks." Gabriel licked his lips. "I like you. I want you in my life, even knowing how your life was before we met." There was nothing else Gabriel could say, but he'd repeat it again and again until Cyn believed him.

Cyn was still thinking about what Gabriel had told him once he was back in his bedroom at Noah's house. He'd known that what Alice had said didn't reflect Gabriel's thoughts about him and that he needed to let this go.

And he was going to.

He might have thought about volunteering at the shelter because he wanted to feel like he was doing something right in his life, but he'd actually enjoyed it. He'd hated seeing people who were having a hard time, but he could do something to help them, and he wanted to continue, even though serving them a meal didn't feel like it was enough. It was *something*, though, and Cyn wasn't going to stop.

He'd been privileged all his life. He'd never realized it, but tonight had slapped that fact in his face, and it was a good thing. He might not enjoy or share all of Alice's opinions of him, but she'd given him the kick in the ass he'd needed. He hadn't even realized it, and he didn't want to think about her words again, but he was becoming a better man thanks to her, and he wanted to resolve things with her. He'd have to do it without Gabriel there, because he knew Gabriel would try to shield and protect both of them, and that was the last thing they needed. They had to talk things out and be honest, and Cyn hoped Alice would be open to that.

He sighed and rolled onto his front. He'd hoped he and Gabriel would be able to spend a little time together that night, maybe drive back to pack territory in the same car, but Gabriel had needed to stay a bit longer to close the shelter and make sure everything was as it should be. Gabriel hadn't said they could still see each other, no doubt because he didn't know how long he'd be still, but even though they wouldn't be spending time together tonight, Cyn felt they'd taken a step forward. He was getting past what Alice had said, and Gabriel obviously didn't care about any of it. They'd make it.

Cyn was sure of it.

The sound of his phone ringing made him smile. He rolled toward his nightstand, expecting the caller to be Gabriel, hopefully wanting to ask Cyn if he was free to spend some time with him.

But it was Cyn's mother.

Cyn sighed. The last thing he wanted was to talk to her, but she'd continue to call until he answered, and there was no way he wanted to spend all night hanging up on her. Besides, given how late it was, Cyn couldn't shake the feeling that maybe something had happened. His mother wasn't the kind of person who would call close to midnight. It shouldn't be done.

"Mother," he said as he answered. He'd probably regret it, but he couldn't ignore it.

"You need to come home."

Cyn sighed. "I already told you—"

"Something happened."

Cyn's breath hitched. "What?"

"It's your father, Cyn. He hasn't been feeling well, and the healer ordered him to stay in bed."

"How bad is it?" Cyn hadn't known his father had health problems, but it wasn't something either of his parents would have told him. He was the child, and that wasn't something he ought to know, or at least, that was the way they thought.

"It's not looking good, although the healer wants to run some more tests. I need you to come home, Cynara."

"Of course. Give me fifteen minutes to pack a bag and tell Noah, and I'll be right there." No matter how his parents had treated him, Cyn wasn't going to turn his back on his parents. He loved them, even if he wasn't sure they loved him.

Noah and his mate were nowhere to be seen, so Cyn scribbled a note and left it on the fridge. He bit his lower lip and wondered what was next. He needed to get home, but he wanted to see Gabriel before he left. He might be home already, or he might not, but when Cyn tried calling him, he didn't answer.

There were no two ways about it. Cyn quickly walked to Gabriel's house, using the path he was starting to know like the back of his hand. The lights were on downstairs, in the living room, and in the kitchen, so Cyn hoped Gabriel was there.

It was Alice who opened the door, though.

Cyn almost groaned at the way she looked him up and down. She leaned against the doorframe and crossed her arms over her chest, arching a brow. "What do you want? Gabriel isn't here yet. You know he's working."

The *unlike you* was implied. Cyn heard it loud and clear. "I know. I was hoping he'd already gotten back."

"Again, what do you want?"

"I have to go back home."

Alice smirked. "Already tired of life without money?"

Cyn gritted his teeth. Now wasn't the moment to get into it with Alice. "Actually, my father is ill. I'm going back to be with him and to support my mother." Cyn knew he should stop there and go, but he wanted to add something first, even though he probably shouldn't. "You know, you have a lot to say about me being spoiled, but you are, too."

Alice's eyes widened. "What the fuck? I'm not spoiled. I ran away when I was thirteen because my stepfather —"

"I know. But you're not thirteen anymore, and *Gabriel* spoils you. You're working hard on your degree, sure, but that's it. You haven't been trying to pay for it yourself very hard."

"Gabriel doesn't want me to." Alice looked like she wanted to strangle Cyn, and Cyn thought that probably wasn't far from the truth.

He felt a bit guilty about throwing that out there and

leaving before he and Alice could talk, but he didn't have time, and she probably needed to think about it. God knew he'd had a lot of time to do that. "You're right. He doesn't want you to worry about money, just like my parents don't want me to worry about it. And I didn't, until now. But I left, even though it meant leaving security behind."

"I'm not going to leave."

"Of course not. Gabriel would be in pieces if you did. But I also don't see you trying to help him. You could talk to Kameron. Gabriel said Kameron would eagerly help you, and I suspect the only reason he hasn't is that Gabriel wants to shoulder all that responsibility. You're an adult, though. You're the one who makes decisions about your life, but I guess you've found it easier to let Gabriel make the hard decisions for you. He's spoiling you. You don't have to think about the economic aspect of your life because he shields you from it like my parents did. I don't think you should judge me for something you do, too."

Cyn turned around and hopped off the porch steps. He wasn't about to face Alice's wrath for what he'd said, even though he thought he was right. He'd have stayed and faced her any other day, but right now, he didn't have the time.

He quickly used the app to contact a Nix and left his GPS on so they'd know where to find him. Once he was home, though, all the righteousness that he'd been feeling disappeared.

He looked at the house where he'd grown up and wondered if it would be the last time that he'd see his father. There was no love lost between them, mostly because of his father and of the way he behaved, but Cyn couldn't imagine life without him. He'd never had to think about it, but now he was confronted with this, and he had no idea how to deal with it. He wished Gabriel could be at his side right now, but Gabriel was at work, where he needed to be.

Cyn could face this on his own. He had to, and while he knew Gabriel would want to support him in this, it was going to have to wait. Hopefully, Cyn could contact Gabriel tomorrow and tell him what had happened. He wasn't sure Alice was going to tell Gabriel, not after what Cyn had said to her. He hoped she would, because he wanted Gabriel to know that he hadn't decided to go home to his parents' money, but either way, he'd need to hear Gabriel's voice after this.

He needed Gabriel in a way he'd never thought possible

Gabriel was exhausted. He always was at this hour of the night after working his two jobs, but his personal life was weighing on him as well now, and he wasn't sure how long he'd be able to shoulder this before he broke.

He'd wanted to go home with Cyn and spend some time with him, but his boss at the shelter had come by, and he'd had to stay to close everything down after talking to her. It was probably too late to call Cyn now. Gabriel remembered the first few days he'd worked at the shelter, and he'd flopped into bed as soon as he got home back then.

The lights were still on in the living room when he got home. Gabriel groaned. He needed to talk to Alice, but God, he didn't want to do that now. He also didn't want to give her the cold shoulder, though, so it looked like they *were* going to do this tonight.

"Alice?" he called out when he walked into the house. He leaned down to untie his shoe and wiggled his toes as soon as they were off. *Better.*

"I'm busy," Alice snapped from the living room.

Gabriel blinked. "What happened?" he asked, walking to the living room.

She was sitting on the couch surrounded by books and notebooks, and she was scowling. It wasn't the first time

Gabriel had found her like that—the stuff she was studying wasn't easy by any means—but there'd been something especially harsh in her voice, and now he wasn't sure he should bring Cyn up. It wasn't going to make Alice happier, that was for sure, although maybe this made it the best moment to do it. She was going to be pissed either way.

Alice huffed. "Nothing."

All right then. "Can I talk to you for a minute?"

"Do you really have to do this right now?"

The answer was no, but Gabriel didn't want to do this at all, and he knew he'd let it go if he didn't do it now. "Yeah. Cyn was at the shelter today," he said, putting down his bag and sitting at the edge of one of the armchairs after moving a book to the coffee table.

Alice scowled. "Don't touch that, and I don't care."

"I don't get what you have against him."

"Didn't we already have this conversation? I don't like him because he's a spoiled brat who doesn't deserve you."

There they were. The exact words Cyn had said about himself—and Gabriel wasn't surprised to hear them from Alice. "You told him that, didn't you?"

"Of course I did." She threw her pen on top of her notebook. "Because it's true. I don't see why I shouldn't have told him. I didn't lie."

"The fact that you think he's a spoiled brat doesn't mean he is one, Alice. He was luckier than both of us, and yes, he's a little immature and naïve, and *spoiled*, but he's a good guy. He volunteered at the shelter tonight. He left his parents and their money. He's trying to grow up and find his own way in life, and having you kick him down again isn't going to help. If you think he's not good enough for me, then why are you trying to stop him from changing?"

Alice's jaw tightened. "Nothing he can do will make him worth your attention."

"He's my mate." Gabriel was hurt and confused. He didn't understand why Alice was so bent on thinking that of Cyn. She hadn't even given him a chance. "And that means that no matter what you think, he *is* the right man for me. And even if he weren't my mate, it wouldn't be your choice to make, would it? It's my life we're talking about, and I'm the one who will make decisions."

"And you decided you need to be with him."

"I *want* to be with him. I'd want it even if he weren't my mate. He's a good guy, Alice, and you'd know that if you'd given him a chance. But you didn't. You haven't even talked to him, not unless it was to tell him all of this. Why can't you at least try?"

Alice got up. Her notebook dropped to the floor, and she didn't pick it up. "I've talked to him more than enough, and none of what he said changed my mind. I won't *ever* think he's good enough for you because he isn't. He's a spoiled brat, and yes, I *do* think that, and he's going to run back to his parents soon if he hasn't done so already. You want to see the best in him because he's your mate, but you're going to end up hurt, and *I'm* going to have to pick up the pieces once he's done with you."

"He's not going to hurt me." Not intentionally. They were both going to hurt each other because that was what everyone in a relationship did. Then they apologized and tried to work things out. But that wasn't the problem Gabriel had with this conversation. "You've never had to pick up the pieces with me. I've never had a relationship so important that I was hurt when it ended. Would asking you to do it one time be too much?"

Alice huffed. "Of course not. I'd do it if I had to. But I don't want to see you hurt, Gabriel."

They were going nowhere with this. "He's *not* going to hurt me, Alice. He's my mate. He's a good guy. He's trying to get his life together, and I'm going to be a part of that life, whether you like it or not. I don't know why you hate him so much, since I'm sure he didn't do anything to you, and at this point, I don't think I want to know. If you can't accept him . . ."

Gabriel didn't want to say it.

"You're going to choose him over me?" Alice asked, her voice steady and cold, so cold that Gabriel didn't think he'd ever heard it that way, at least not directed toward him.

"I don't want to have to do it. I don't care if you hate Cyn, as long as you accept that he's in my life and that he's not going anywhere. But you don't seem to want to do that, and while I hate the thought of not having you in my life, and the fact that you're making me choose even though I don't want to, *you* are the one who won't even try. He wants to. *He* doesn't want me to choose. He doesn't want me to have to make that choice. You don't seem to care, though, and I can't believe you want me to."

Alice opened her mouth, but she didn't say anything. She snatched one of the books from the coffee table—Gabriel didn't think she even paid attention to which one it was—and stomped out of the living room and up the stairs. He heard her slam her bedroom door, and he slid back against the armchair.

That could have gone better, although he wasn't sure how. Alice had something against Cyn, and as far as Gabriel could see, it wasn't something rational. Gabriel wasn't sure how to fix that. He'd always helped Alice when she needed him, and since something was wrong, he wanted to help this time too. He had no idea how, though, and she wasn't going to talk to him.

Was he going to have to choose between his best friend—his sister—and his mate? How was he supposed to do that? He cared for both of them, and Cyn had done nothing wrong. It would be easier to decide if he had.

Gabriel sighed and slid his phone out of his pocket. He texted Cyn, then stared at the screen of his phone, but the little ticks didn't turn blue. Cyn was probably asleep, so Gabriel wasn't surprised, but he wished his mate was there. He had no idea how to behave or even how to feel about what was going on with Alice, and while Cyn probably wouldn't, either, he'd at least help him feel better.

Gabriel wasn't angry, just clueless and sad. He wanted the two most important people in his life to get along, and he had no idea where to start to make that happen.

"Thank you," Cyn told the Nix who'd shimmered him to the front of the gate.

The Nix nodded and shimmered away, leaving Cyn alone. Cyn wanted to call him back, because the thought of facing what was waiting for him alone was nerve-wracking, but of course, he didn't. He didn't even know the guy, and the person he wanted was Gabriel, not a guy he didn't know. But Gabriel was still at work, and Cyn didn't want to bother him. He'd call later, once he knew what was happening and how long he'd need to stay.

There was no use delaying this, was there? He really didn't want to see his parents, because he knew his mother would at least try to convince him to move back home. He didn't know if his father would have the energy to nag him, but his mother no doubt would, and Cyn wasn't ready to face that. He supposed he never would be, and that was okay. This wasn't his home anymore. He was only there to visit, and when his father was better, he'd go home to Gabriel and Noah, and hopefully, to a job with Oliver since Oliver had hinted at it tonight.

He used his remote to open the gate and snuck through. The lights were on downstairs, but not in his parents' bedroom, so maybe his father was sleeping. Cyn supposed that was a good thing. His father needed rest, right? It would help him get better.

His mother opened the door before he could climb the stone steps. She looked the way she had when he'd left, and it gave Cyn pause, although only for a moment. Of course his mother looked good. She always did because it wouldn't be a good thing to show the world — or even her son — that she was worried.

"I wasn't sure you'd come," she said.

"Of course I'd come. Father is ill."

She wrinkled her nose and let Cyn walk into the entrance. She closed the door behind him, the sound loud in the mostly empty space. "He's in the living room," she said.

Cyn blinked. "In the living room?" He'd expected his father to be in bed. From what his mother had said, he was gravely ill, so it would have made sense.

"He's waiting for you. We both were. Why don't you give me your bag?"

Cyn frowned. "It's not a bother. How is he? What did the healer say?"

"Let's go sit with him."

Cyn expected a lot of things — to find his father looking older, sick, maybe even to find him stretched out on the couch in his pajamas, something that had never happened in their house — but not what he found when he stepped into the living room.

His father looked like he always did. His tail was tightly wound around his waist, and he was wearing a suit, complete with tie and jacket. His back was ramrod straight as he sat in his armchair, and he rose when he saw Cyn. "Cynara."

Cyn looked from his father to his mother. "What's going on?"

"You should hand your bag and your cell phone to your mother."

"What?"

A noise behind him made him turn around. His eyes widened at the sight of two men—not demons since they didn't have tails and the swirling marks on their exposed skins, but probably not human, either.

"What's going on?" he asked. "Mother said you were sick. I came to help . . . to check on you."

"I'm perfectly fine, but we needed to find a way to get you to come home."

They'd lied. Cyn wasn't sure how he hadn't realized it earlier. He'd been so focused on his father's health and the possibility of losing him that he hadn't even thought about it.

He turned around and headed for the door. "I'm leaving. I can't believe you did this. Telling me you were ill, implying that you might die . . ." Cyn was disgusted, both with his parents and with himself. How could he have been so naïve? He'd known they didn't want him to leave, that they wanted him to obey their orders.

"You're not going anywhere, Cynara," his mother snapped in an uncharacteristic sign of anger. "We're not going to allow you to ruin our lives and your future the way you've been trying to."

"I'm not ruining anything." Cyn's heart was racing. He needed to get out of there, but somehow, he doubted he was going to be allowed to. Now the reason for those two guys' presence was clear.

"Not anymore. These two gentlemen will make sure you don't leave the house."

"You can't keep me a prisoner in the house."

"A prisoner, no, but we can make sure you don't make any more mistakes. We already contacted your fiancée, and her father agreed to speed up the wedding. You will be getting married two days from now."

Cyn was going to throw up all over his mother's Persian

carpet. He was grateful for the fact that Noah hadn't told her Cyn had met his mate. He knew she wouldn't care about that—demons didn't have mates, and even if they did, the wealthy ones who wanted to preserve family names and all that crap would ignore it anyway. They'd be horrified if their mates didn't belong to the same social circle as they did. So he was pretty sure being Gabriel's mate wouldn't mean anything to his parents. It certainly wouldn't be a reason for them to allow him to go back to Gillham. Nothing would convince them that it was a good idea, especially not Gabriel's presence in Cyn's life.

But Cyn had to try. If there was only one chance his parents would relent if they found out about Gabriel, Cyn had to tell them.

"I don't want to get married. I have a mate."

His mother did that wrinkling her nose again. "A *mate*? Oh, Cynara. Did you let someone fool you into thinking that you had a mate? You're a demon. We don't have mates."

"That doesn't mean I'm not Gabriel's mate." Cyn knew Gabriel hadn't lied. He didn't have a reason to.

His mother waved his words away. "No matter. Whether you are his mate or not, you are engaged, and you'll be getting married in two days. Please give your phone to one of these gentlemen, and don't even think about trying to sneak out. They're werewolves. They'll know, and they'll bring you back. I don't want you to have visible bruises, though."

Cyn didn't want to marry his fiancée—he hadn't even met her, for fuck's sake—but it might be the best way for him to get out of there. The sense of betrayal when he thought of Gabriel made his stomach churn, though.

He didn't want to comply with his parents, even if he was only faking it. He wanted them to know he hated this, that he hated *them* for what they were doing to him. They wouldn't care, not as long as they got what they wanted, but it was the least Cyn could do. "I won't marry her."

"You will if you know what's good for you," his father said. There was barely restrained anger in his voice. "We hired security to make sure you don't leave and that none of your *friends* come in. You'll be here the day after tomorrow, wearing the clothes your mother picked for you, and you *will* say yes when you're asked if you take that girl as your wife."

"You can't make me say yes."

"Maybe not, but I *can* make sure you don't leave your bedroom until you comply. If you want to be a prisoner in your own home, then it will be your choice."

And no one would come for him.

Or maybe they would. He'd left a note for Noah, so even if Alice didn't tell Gabriel where Cyn had gone, Noah would know. He'd start to worry if he didn't get news from Cyn in a few days. Hopefully, he'd be there before Cyn was forced to marry the girl his parents had chosen for him, but if he wasn't, Cyn would take being a prisoner in the bedroom over marrying a woman he'd never seen.

"Take him upstairs," Cyn's father said.

Big hands wrapped around Cyn's arms. He tried to pull away, to resist, but he didn't stand a chance next to those two werewolves. One of them shoved his hand into Cyn's jeans and took his phone out. Cyn watched him hand it over to his mother, and he knew he wouldn't see that phone again. At least it was locked. His mother didn't know his password, so she wouldn't be able to get to the texts he'd exchanged with Gabriel. Still, it felt like a lifeline was taken away from him, and Cyn fought harder, smacking one of the wolves across the face with his tail. The guy jerked back and growled, but he didn't raise his hands to Cyn.

Cyn's mother needed him unmarred for the wedding. She hadn't been kidding about that, and Cyn had the childish impulse to continue fighting so he'd get beat up. Let his mother explain *that* to his in-laws.

He needed to be smarter, though. Noah and Gabriel were going to come for him, and he'd have to be able to leave on his own two feet when they did.

CHAPTER SIX

Gabriel was worried. He probably shouldn't be — two days wasn't a long time, even though it was Cyn he was thinking about. But two days without hearing from him still didn't sit right with Gabriel, and he wasn't sure what to do.

Had something happened? Cyn hadn't come to the shelter yesterday, and his phone was off. He hadn't answered any of Gabriel's texts. Even when he'd been distant after Alice had gotten to him, he'd answered, and they'd gotten past that. *Right?*

Something was going on. Gabriel could feel it. His skunk could feel it, and it wanted to find Cyn and tear apart whoever was keeping him away from them. If they'd been bonded, Gabriel would have known something was wrong from the start, but they hadn't even talked about it. They hadn't gone further than a few kisses and handholding because Cyn was dealing with a lot, turning his life around and getting his bearings, and Gabriel hadn't wanted to push. Cyn was only nineteen, and he had no idea how to live away from his parents.

Gabriel poked at the screen of his phone again, but there were no new messages, nothing.

Doubts slithered in. Had Alice been right when she'd said maybe Cyn had already had enough of not having access to his parents' money? Gabriel didn't want to believe it, but maybe he should.

He jerked up into a sitting position. *No.* He wasn't going to let Alice's words get to him. Even if Cyn had decided to go back, and Gabriel didn't think he had, there was no way he wouldn't have told Gabriel about it. He'd have at least texted, yet he hadn't. It was like he'd disappeared from the face of the earth ever since he'd left the shelter two nights ago, and Gabriel had enough of waiting and giving him time. If Cyn was sulking, Gabriel wanted to know. At least he could stop freaking out and give Cyn the space he needed if that was what he wanted.

Gabriel hopped off the couch and stumbled on the leg of the coffee table in his rush to get to his shoes by the front door. He shoved his feet into them and leaned down to tie them.

"You're going out?" Alice asked. She was in the kitchen doorframe watching him.

Things between them were tense. They hadn't talked since they'd fought the night Gabriel had confronted her. They were both careful around each other, and Gabriel didn't have the time right now. "Yeah."

"He hasn't called?"

"Not yet, no." And she knew it. Gabriel had no doubt Alice had been keeping an eye on him, probably to gloat when Cyn didn't come around. Gabriel wouldn't have thought that of her before, but right now, he wasn't sure she wouldn't do exactly that.

"You should let it go."

"I'm not in the mood, Alice." Gabriel knew something was wrong. He could feel it, and he didn't want to listen to her making fun of him or trying to convince him otherwise.

"Gabriel—"

"No. I'm going to go over to Cyn's house and check in with his cousin. I'll let you know if something happened."

She looked at her feet and bit her lower lip. Gabriel wondered if she was gearing up to another fight, so he rushed out the door, not even stopping to grab a jacket. He wasn't going to need one anyway. Cyn's house wasn't far.

Alice called out, but Gabriel ignored her and rushed into

the woods. He followed the path he knew well by now, his heart in his throat, the need to get to his mate eating at him. He shouldn't have ignored the feeling that something was wrong for so long. What if something had happened to Cyn and it was too late? Gabriel had no way to know if Cyn was okay, if he was even alive, although that wasn't something he wanted to consider. He had to believe that Cyn was okay, maybe in trouble, but not so bad that Gabriel wouldn't be able to help him. And Gabriel was going to try. He was going to do whatever he had to to get Cyn back.

If he wasn't ignoring Gabriel, of course. There was a chance that Cyn had decided he didn't want Gabriel in his life, and Gabriel was going to have to accept that, but not before he at least tried to talk to his mate.

He was out of breath by the time he got to Noah's house. He knocked on the door and tried to catch his breath, rubbing the sweat off his forehead. He swallowed when the door swung open.

"Gabriel?" Noah asked. He frowned. "Has something happened to Cyn?"

Gabriel sucked in a breath. "I don't know. That's why I'm here. Do you know where he is?"

"I thought he was with you. He wasn't home when Duncan and I came home after our date the other night. We thought he was with you. I was annoyed because he hadn't let me know, but his phone has been off."

Gabriel shook his head. "I haven't seen him since that same night at the shelter. I had to stay to work late, but he came home. I've been trying to call him, too, but without success. I hoped he was here or that you'd be able to tell me what was going on."

Noah swore and stepped away from the door. Gabriel walked in and closed it, following Noah to the kitchen, where Duncan stood in front of the stove cooking something that smelled heavenly yet made Gabriel want to throw up.

Cyn had been gone for two whole days and nights. They had no idea where he was or what had happened to him, and no way to find him.

"Noah?" Duncan asked.

"Cyn's gone."

"Gone?"

"Yes. He wasn't with Gabriel."

Duncan put down his wooden spoon. "And neither of you have heard from him?"

"No."

"Well, we know he came home since he ate dinner and left the plate in the dishwasher. That means he left again, for whatever reason. He didn't call you, Gabriel?"

"No."

Duncan turned to the fridge. "We didn't check for messages."

"Because he'd have called if he needed anything," Noah pointed out.

"Or maybe he knew we were on a date, and he didn't want to bother us." Duncan leaned forward and snatched a pink piece of paper from the fridge. "There. It says his mother called and that his father is sick."

Gabriel tensed. "He went home?"

"Looks like he did."

It made sense. Even though Cyn's relationship with his parents was rocky, who wouldn't run when told their father was sick? "I don't understand why he didn't let me know."

"You weren't home. You were working. I think he didn't want to bother you, either."

Alice had been home, but she hadn't said anything about Cyn, except for asking Gabriel what he was going to do if Cyn had gone home. *Dammit.* She'd known, hadn't she? "Why hasn't he called either of us, though?" He couldn't think about what Alice might have or not have done right now. He had to focus on Cyn.

"It could simply be that he's spending time with his parents," Duncan suggested.

Noah snorted. "He's probably going crazy already. And even if my uncle is sick, there's no way Cyn wouldn't let us know something, especially Gabriel. No, something is going on."

"You don't think he's home?"

"I don't see why he should have lied to us. But maybe he went home, and something happened, and he hasn't been able to contact us. There *has* to be a reason. I don't think he's able to call, and I don't like that."

"Would his parents hurt him?" Gabriel asked. His throat felt dry as dust.

"Physically, I don't think so, although I haven't had contact with them in almost fifteen years. But from what Cyn has told me, I think they were abusing him emotionally, and since he hasn't called, well, something is definitely wrong. They might not have allowed him to call, which means he's stuck there and needs help."

Duncan groaned. "You need to get Kameron."

"I don't need Kameron. We're just going to check in on my sick uncle, right?"

"Noah."

"No, Duncan. This is a family matter, and it's not like my aunt and uncle are drug dealers or whatever. They probably locked him in his bedroom or something, and that's something we can solve without involving the big guns."

Gabriel hoped he was right, because he wasn't waiting for Kameron or anyone else to step in. He was leaving as soon as he managed to get a lift from a Nix.

Cyn glared at his locked bedroom door, then at the clothes that hung on the door of his walk-in closet. His mother had left them there last night and had told him to be ready at ten the next morning, so of course, he'd put on his oldest pair of jeans and a t-shirt with holes, and he hadn't combed his hair. His mother was going to be pissed, and he wanted her to be. He wanted her to know that she was forcing him into this. Everyone there would know as soon as they saw him.

He hoped the two bulky werewolves weren't going to try to strip him and dress him up like he was a doll. He could see them do it if his parents ordered them to, but he'd rather stay as far away as possible from them as he could.

The door opened without warning. Cyn kept his scowl in place and looked up at werewolf one. They hadn't bothered telling him their names, and he didn't want to know them. "What?" he snapped.

"Your parents are waiting for you downstairs." The man's gaze flickered to the suit hanging on the door, but he didn't say anything.

Good.

Cyn stood from his bed—he was pretty sure werewolf one would haul him up and carry him downstairs if he didn't co-operate—and followed the man into the hallway. He wasn't surprised when they ended up in his father's office, or at the way his parents looked at him. They'd noticed his clothes and his defiance. It wouldn't do much in the end, not if no one came to rescue Cyn, but at least he wasn't laying down and taking it. His parents might be forcing him to do what they wanted, but he wasn't going to take it the way he had before. He had something to fight for now—his new life, the job Oliver had offered him, *Gabriel.*

God, Gabriel. What was he thinking? Had Alice explained what had happened, or did Gabriel think Cyn had left him and everything he'd been trying to build? Cyn wasn't sure he would put it past Alice to lie and leave out the fact that Cyn had thought his father was ill.

"I see you aren't wearing the clothes I chose for you," his mother said.

"I'm not."

"Why are you making this so difficult, Cynara? You had everything—a beautiful house, as much money as you could ever want, a bright future with your father at work, a gorgeous wife and the possibility of children. You had the respect of our peers. People looked up at you. Why are you bent on destroying everything your father and I have worked so hard to build?"

"I'm not trying to destroy anything. I want to make my own life, that's all. Don't you want me to be happy?"

She stiffened. "You can be happy with what we're giving you."

"But I can't, Mother. I thought I could, and I tried. I went to the school you wanted me to go to. I spent time with the people you wanted me to be with. I didn't say anything when you chose a woman for me to marry. But I can't do this anymore. I'm not happy, and I won't be, not if I follow the path you've created for me."

"Enough," Cyn's father snapped. "Happiness has nothing to do with this. As my son, you have rules to follow and expectations to fulfill, and you will as you're told. I am *not* going to allow you to behave like one of those animals you seem to like so much."

Werewolf two, who had been in the office when Cyn and werewolf one had walked in, grunted. Cyn's father didn't seem to realize that he'd insulted the huge bodyguards he'd hired, although that probably didn't matter. They weren't going to kick his ass, not if they wanted to be paid.

Cyn swallowed. The only time he'd defied his parents had been the day he'd left home, and they hadn't expected it. They'd thought he was talking out of his ass and that he wouldn't have the courage to do what he was saying.

But he'd *had* that courage. He'd left, and he'd found his way to Gillham. He'd found a job and a mate. He'd been happy, and he could still be. There was no way for his parents to *make* him say yes to this wedding, no matter what they thought. He doubted they'd invited many people, but they'd had to have invited someone. They couldn't have their son get married without their friends there, not if they wanted to avoid people talking behind their backs. So there would be a small crowd there to watch, and there was no way Cyn was saying yes, not to anyone who wasn't Gabriel.

"Did you hear me, Cynara? You are going to do what you're told, and you're going to do it with a smile on your face. You might not care for your own safety, but I looked into your *mate* after you mentioned him, and I can make his life difficult."

Cyn's stomach dropped. "What?" he croaked.

"That man has debts. Two jobs. He might be a part of that pack, but that doesn't mean I can't get to him, and I will if I have to. I'll ruin him, make sure he can't find work anymore and that he has to reimburse all his debts in one go."

Cyn had to think instead of panicking. It was true that his father had a lot of powerful friends, and he could probably do everything he'd threatened himself, but he wouldn't be able to touch Gabriel, not in Gillham, not when Gabriel was a Gillham pack member. Kameron Rhett would never allow a pack member to get hurt, either physically or in the way Cyn's father had described.

Cyn's father wanted him to panic and to give in, but the only person he could hurt was Cyn himself. Gabriel was safe, and he would continue to be safe. Cyn didn't have to give in for his sake.

He still hoped someone was coming for him, though. He could stand up to his parents, but things weren't going to get better until he managed to get out. Even if he said no and humiliated them in front of their friends and business associates, it didn't mean they'd kick him out, as much as he wanted them to. No, they'd try to get Cyn in the long run, lock him into his bedroom again and promise him he could leave once he was married and ready to obey them

"You're going to go back upstairs and put on the suit your mother chose for you. Your fiancée will be here in an hour. You'll be ready to come downstairs and wait for her in front of the celebrant. You'll marry her. I won't take no for an answer. If you aren't married by the end of the day, your shifter friend will face the consequences, and you know I'm not bluffing."

He wasn't, but he didn't understand that he wouldn't be able to hurt Gabriel. He didn't understand what a true family was. He couldn't, not when he'd never even loved his only son.

Cyn could see that now. To his parents, he was nothing more than a puppet. They didn't love him, and doing what they wanted wouldn't change that. Once Cyn was out of there, he'd never come back, and he'd never see them again. He didn't want to. He loved them, but that love wasn't going to influence him anymore. He wouldn't let it. His parents didn't deserve it.

But Gabriel did. He deserved all the love Cyn could give him, and Cyn was going to make it work with him. He didn't care if he had to apologize to Alice and beg her to accept him. He'd do it if it made Gabriel happy. He'd do pretty much anything for him.

Cyn's father nodded at werewolf one. "Take him to his bedroom and make sure he changes."

"Sir?" the man asked.

Cyn's father shook his head. "I don't care how you manage it, as long as you don't leave marks on him. I expect him to be dressed in his suit an hour from now, and you'll make sure he is unless you want your pay to be halved."

Well, shit. That wasn't going to be fun, was it? Cyn didn't want to obey and to dress up for this farce of a wedding, but if he had to choose between that and facing whatever werewolf one was going to throw at him, maybe he should go the easy way, even if it meant giving in at least on this.

"What the fuck?" Noah muttered. He pushed a strand of his long blue hair away from his face and peered at the house in front of them.

The gate was open, letting in a steady stream of luxurious cars. They were greeted at the front door by a guy that might have been a butler, and the people were led inside. They were all dressed to the nines as if they were going to some kind of party.

And Cyn was somewhere in there. He had to be. "Do your aunt and uncle often throw parties?" Gabriel asked, unsure what to think.

"No. They don't like parties, as far as I know. The only reason they go to parties is to show off and to make their friends jealous, or something like that. This doesn't make sense."

"Maybe Cyn's father is better and they want to celebrate."

Noah straightened his back. "I have no idea what's going on, but we're going to find out." He looked down at himself, wrinkled his nose, and shrugged. "We're not dressed for the occasion, but I don't think that's going to be a problem." With that, he strode toward the gate, and Gabriel scrambled to follow him.

He'd thought about the life Cyn had left behind, of course, but he hadn't quite pictured this. The lawn was perfect, not one stand of grass out of place. The rose bushes looked like they'd rather spontaneously combust than to grow out of the shape they all had.

And the house. It was huge and looked like it belonged in the English countryside — not that Gabriel had ever even been to the UK, but he'd watched enough episodes of that historical drama set there.

The butler eyed them as they walked along the driveway. He didn't give a hint as to what he was thinking, not even when Noah stopped in front of him. "Hello. My invitation got lost in the mail, but I'm sure my aunt and uncle would have wanted me here."

The butler's eyebrow twitched. "I'm sorry, sir, but I can't let you in without an invitation."

"Aww, come on. I don't want to miss this." He leaned closer. "Even though I'm not quite sure what *this* is. I don't think my aunt and uncle have ever thrown a party."

The butler cleared his throat. "I suppose it's not every day their only son gets married. Now if you'll excuse me. I need you to leave, or I'll have to call security."

Cyn was getting married? He had to be. He was their only child, and this guy had said that his parents' only son was getting married.

But Cyn didn't want to get married. They'd talked about it, and Gabriel knew it was what his parents expected from him, which was one of the reasons Cyn had left home. He didn't want to bind his life to a woman he'd never met. He wanted to marry for love, maybe bond now that Gabriel had found him and realized they were mates. There was no way he was doing this of his own volition, and that meant he was being forced to get married, that he was probably held prisoner somewhere in this house.

"Calm down," Noah murmured, grabbing Gabriel's arm and pulling him back to the street.

"They're forcing him," Gabriel managed to choke out.

"I know, but we're not going to let that happen. We need

to regroup, okay? But don't let anyone see how shocked and anxious you are over this. We don't want to clue them in on what we're about to do."

"*What* are we about to do?"

Noah grinned. "We're about to break Cyn out of the house, of course."

Gabriel followed Noah since he didn't have a clue where to start with this. Noah seemed to, though, so the best for everyone would probably be if Gabriel followed his orders.

Noah eyed the house again. "You know, I don't think subtlety is going to work here," he said.

"What do you mean?"

"Well, my aunt and uncle are going to try again if we don't make sure they know that Cyn isn't going to marry the women they chose for him. They'll try to guilt him into it, or maybe they'll fake another illness. No, the best way to do this is to make it obvious to them that their best option is to stay away from Cyn, maybe disinherit him or something. That way Cyn will be free of them."

"And how do we do that?"

"Mmm. Are you ready to face their wrath?"

"I'll do anything I have to do to get Cyn out of there."

"That's what I hoped you'd say."

Noah strode up the driveway again. The butler was busy greeting yet another elegant couple, and he took a double-take when he saw them. He stepped forward, but Noah ignored him, hopping up the stone steps and through the front door as if he belonged there. Gabriel supposed Noah did, but *he* certainly didn't, and he couldn't help but look around as he followed Noah.

"What are you doing? Sir!" the butler said, his voice not quite a yell.

Gabriel knew who Cyn's parents were without asking. They were standing at the bottom of a huge staircase, greeting their guests with plastic smiles on their faces. They looked up at the commotion, and Cyn's mother looked like she'd been presented with a dead spider or something.

"Noah. You weren't invited," she said, her voice cold and slightly disgusted.

"I wasn't. And here I thought my invitation got lost. I expected to be invited to Cyn's wedding."

"*Cynara* doesn't want to see you. Neither do I."

Her husband nodded, and a huge guy that had to be security stepped forward. He grabbed Gabriel's arm and pulled, but Gabriel stood his ground. He wasn't there to antagonize these people, just to rescue his mate, and he didn't care how they felt about it.

"That's bullshit," Noah snapped, his fake smile slipping from his face. "Cyn's been living with my mate and me, and I know what he wants and doesn't want. He's not going to marry this girl, no matter how much you threaten him. He's not even going to get to see her, because Gabriel and I are leaving, and we're taking him with us."

The security guy pulled harder on Gabriel's arm, and Gabriel had enough. He jerked toward him and growled, the shift coming over him before he could think about it. He needed his skunk, and his skunk was coming out because they were going to save their mate, damn it.

He dropped on his four feet and snapped his teeth at the security guy, hissing and stamping his foot when he reached for him again. Now that he was in his skunk form and that he wasn't distracted, he could smell that the guy was a werewolf. There was no way he could take on a werewolf, not even in his animal form, not physically at least. That didn't mean he was going to back down, though.

The werewolf laughed, and Gabriel struck. He threw himself forward and dug his teeth into the guy's leg, then, when the guy howled and tried to grab him by the tail, he twisted and sprayed him.

The werewolf stumbled back. Gabriel didn't often use his spray, but he knew its effect on people. It was strong enough to irritate the eyes, and that was what he needed. Noah yelled, "Upstairs!" and Gabriel ran up the steps, ignoring the smell and the yelling. The people down there were a mess, running away from the smell and coughing.

Gabriel had never minded being a skunk shifter. People didn't usually take him seriously because he was small and cute, but that didn't mean he couldn't defend himself.

Once up the stairs, he had no idea where to go. He could smell his spray from there, but when he focused, he managed to get a hint of Cyn's scent, and he followed it. The hallways felt like a maze, but that wasn't a bad thing. It meant Gabriel was able to lose himself in them and to hide when the security guard—another one—tried to catch him. It was confusing, though, and it took him too long to get to the door he thought opened into Cyn's bedroom.

"He's in here," Noah said, startling Gabriel.

Gabriel blinked up at him, and Noah leaned down and scratched the top of Gabriel's head. "That was brilliant. They're all still running around trying to air the room. We don't have much time, though."

Gabriel nodded. Noah straightened and opened the door.

Cyn knew something was happening downstairs, but he had no idea what it was. He could open his bedroom door and go check, but he didn't want to give his mother the satisfaction. He couldn't be sure this wasn't something she'd organized.

He hadn't yet put on his suit. Werewolf one had glared at him, but he'd been called downstairs, and after a growled threat, he'd left. Cyn had no intention of changing. His mother would have to have him dragged to the altar in his worn jeans and holey t-shirt if she wanted him there, and even then, he was *not* going to marry that girl.

He fully expected his mother to come in when the bedroom door opened, but instead, Noah rushed in, followed by a . . . skunk?

"Noah?" Cyn croaked. He couldn't look away from the skunk. There was no way it was a real skunk, and he knew Gabriel was a skunk shifter. He'd wanted to see, but he'd never asked. He didn't want to make Gabriel feel like he had to shift or like he was a curiosity, even though he kind of was.

Noah grinned. "Hey there. We got worried when you didn't call."

Cyn allowed his shoulders to slump. "They took my phone."

"I'll buy you a new one, don't worry. Do you have to pack before we leave?"

Cyn hadn't unpacked his backpack. He hadn't wanted to do that because it would have felt like he was surrendering, giving up hope. "No. They're not going to let us leave, though."

Noah leaned down and patted Gabriel on the head. "Your guy here is an asset, although I suggest you try not to breathe too deeply when we get to the entrance." He opened his arms. "And he's not the only asset. You're too young for your powers to have emerged yet, but I'm not. I'll make them explode if they so much as try to stop us." He frowned. "Or maybe I'll start with a vase or something."

"You're not the only one with that power, and there is werewolf security," Cyn pointed out.

"Yeah, but they won't want their friends and associates to see this. They're not going to want to lose their respect or whatever. It's already going to be hard enough for them to have all those people watch as their son leaves instead of marrying whatever girl they chose. They're not going to want to make it worse, trust me."

He was right. This was going to be a scandal as it was. It would only be worse if his parents tried to stop him. If he was the only one making a spectacle of himself, their reputations would be tarnished, but they'd be safe, and they could rebuild them. If *they* were the ones to snap, though, nothing would help them get back to where they'd been before. Doing this meant cutting ties with them, though, and never coming back.

Cyn was more than ready to do that.

He grabbed his backpack. "Let's go."

Noah nodded and left the bedroom, but before following him, Cyn took the time to stop and crouch next to Gabriel. He gently touched Gabriel's head, and Gabriel tilted his head and closed his eyes in what Cyn hoped was pleasure at his touch. "Thanks for coming for me." They'd need to talk once this was over, but they'd have time to do it later. Right now, Cyn needed to face his parents one last time.

He was nervous. He wasn't going to change his mind, but they were still his parents, and this felt final more than the first time he'd left. He knew his parents wouldn't be calling him anymore, and that they probably wouldn't try luring him home again. That was okay. Cyn wouldn't have to worry about it again, and he didn't think he'd ever be able to forgive what they'd done.

He was ready, no matter how unsure he felt.

He opened his arms, and Gabriel scrambled up his chest. He knew Gabriel wasn't going to spray him, so he held him close, taking comfort in the warm, furry weight that clung to him. Gabriel might not be human right now, and he might not be able to comfort Cyn the way he would as a human, but that didn't mean he wasn't there for him.

Cyn followed Noah into the hallway, then down the stairs to the entrance. The place was a mess. All the windows had been opened, and one of the security guards his parents had hired was sitting in a chair with his eyes red and watering. The only other people there were Cyn's parents, and he raised his chin as he prepared to face them. Gabriel rubbed his nose against Cyn's jaw, silently telling him he wasn't alone.

He'd *never* be alone again, and that was all he'd ever wanted.

"Where do you think you're going?" Cyn's mother asked as she stepped closer. She reached out, but she didn't touch him. He couldn't remember the last time she had. They'd never been a warm and cuddling family.

"I'm leaving. I'm going home."

"This is your home."

"It's not. It has never been. It was a house I shared with you, nothing more." But Cyn had found home now, with Gabriel and Noah and Duncan, and with the friends he'd been making.

"We're not going to allow you to—" his father started.

"You're not going to allow me anything. I'm leaving, and that's final." Cyn could see people peeking in from the open windows and the doors. He was glad for their presence, even though he didn't like it. They meant his parents wouldn't throw a fit.

"Cynara." His mother's voice was shrill. "If you leave now, if you do this to us, you won't be welcome here ever again. You won't be our son."

Cyn swallowed. "I know." And he was doing it anyway.

His exit wasn't dramatic. He stepped out of the entrance, leaving his old life behind, and followed Noah toward a Nix who was waiting for them at the gate. He didn't look back. He didn't want to, and he didn't need to. He had everything he needed already—Gabriel in his arms, Noah waiting for him, a home in Gillham. No matter how much it hurt, leaving his parents was the right thing to do, the only decision Cyn would be able to live with.

The Nix didn't ask questions, shimmering them straight into Noah's living room and leaving. Duncan was there, and he rushed to Noah's side while Gabriel shifted in Cyn's arms.

Cyn dropped his bag and grabbed a blanket from the couch, wrapping it around Gabriel's naked body. Gabriel didn't seem to notice—he pushed himself between Cyn's arms, and Cyn relaxed at his familiar scent.

"I was terrified," Gabriel murmured, his breath warm against the skin of Cyn's neck.

Cyn nodded and buried his face in Gabriel's hair. "Me, too. I didn't know if you'd realize something had happened or if you'd think I'd left. After what I told Alice, I'm not surprised she didn't tell you."

Gabriel leaned back, frowning. "Alice?"

"I came by the other night. I was hoping you were home even though I knew you had to work late. She was there, and I told her my mother had called to tell me my father was ill." Cyn grimaced. "I also told her that she's as spoiled as me, since she's letting you pay for her college degree without trying too hard to convince you otherwise. I get why she didn't tell you anything."

"I'm going to kill her," Gabriel growled. He stepped away, but Cyn grabbed his arm and pulled him against his chest again. "Later? I thought I'd lost you."

Gabriel snuggled against Cyn again. "Later," he agreed.

"Why don't the two of you go upstairs?" Noah asked. "Duncan and I will go to the grocery store and get lunch ready. I bet you have a lot of stuff to tell us, Cyn."

Noah wasn't as sly as he probably thought he was, but Cyn was glad for the time alone with Gabriel. He needed it. They both did. "Sounds good, thanks."

"Just, keep things to your room, yeah?" Duncan asked. Noah slapped his arm, but it was okay. Cyn wasn't offended.

He did need some alone time with Gabriel. He was done being afraid and waiting. He was done doing what other people thought he should do.

He wanted Gabriel. He *trusted* Gabriel, and he knew they were both in this forever. What did it matter if they bonded later or now? It was no one's business but theirs, and while they did need to talk about it, Cyn had made his decision.

He wanted to bond with Gabriel and be with him for the rest of their long lives, and no one was going to stop him.

CHAPTER SEVEN

This was what heaven was like. It had to be, right? Because it certainly felt like heaven, and Gabriel had never thought he'd think of sex that way.

Cyn pushed into Gabriel, slow and steady and infuriating, and Gabriel clung to his shoulders. He never wanted to let go, especially not after almost losing him. He *was* never letting go, and Cyn's question about them bonding flitted through Gabriel's mind.

They hadn't made a decision, but the yearning to bind them forever never left Gabriel, and it was especially strong in moments like these in which from two, they became one.

"Do it, Gabe," Cyn murmured. He stopped moving once he was entirely inside of Gabriel, and Gabriel wrapped himself around him, clutching his hips with his thighs and hooking his feet together on the small of Cyn's back.

"We should talk about it first," Gabriel murmured. It was hard to focus when Cyn was gently rolling his hips and driving Gabriel crazy.

Cyn was a good lover. He made sure Gabriel was okay with what they were doing and that he came before focusing on himself. Gabriel wasn't used to it, but the knowledge that he could have it for the rest of his life — and along with it, the love and affection, the friendship and support — helped. He wanted to give in and bite Cyn, but he couldn't help the niggle of doubt that Cyn might regret it.

Cyn leaned back and looked Gabriel in the eyes. "Do it, Gabe. I want it. We both do."

"You're young." Gabriel needed to think, but Cyn was making it hard, and Gabriel had no doubt he was doing it on purpose.

Cyn's tail stroked against Gabriel's side and wiggled between them to wrap around Gabriel's dick. "So? I'll be twenty next month. We've been together for months. We're mates. I'm not going to change my mind or regret it. I love you. You're it for me, and I don't want to wait."

Gabriel sagged. "Now isn't exactly the best moment to have this conversation," he groaned. The slide of Cyn's cock inside him was distracting, dammit.

"We don't need to have this conversation." Cyn pushed harder into Gabriel, and Gabriel had to focus hard to follow what he was saying. "We both want to bond. Don't let your doubts and fears take over. They might be there, but they're wrong, and they don't matter. What matters is that we love each other and that we both want the same thing."

He was right. They did. Gabriel knew that even without talking to Cyn about it. They'd been through a lot since Cyn had arrived in Gillham, but they'd always been there for each other, and nothing was going to change that.

On Cyn's next thrust into him, Gabriel surged, his fangs already out. Cyn didn't act surprised. Instead, he canted his head to the side as he continued to move inside Gabriel, and Gabriel felt his rhythm falter when his fangs sank into his neck.

He paused, Cyn's blood filling his mouth, waiting for Cyn to do something, maybe push him away and tell him he'd changed his mind, but instead, Cyn cradled Gabriel closer and gently pushed his face more tightly against his neck in an obvious sign that he was okay with this.

Gabriel drank.

Cyn's blood was hot and tasted metallic, but it was easy to ignore how the taste made Gabriel's stomach roil. Gabriel was bonding them together, and he didn't care if Cyn's blood tasted like mushrooms.

"That feels way better than it should," Cyn murmured. He tightened his hands on Gabriel's thighs, and his tail moved faster around Gabriel's cock.

Gabriel was about to come, but he wanted Cyn to be there with him. He'd been told how the pleasure of bonding during sex could be amplified by bonding at the right moment, and they only had one shot at this.

He managed to shift a nail into a claw—and almost stabbed Cyn in the side with it—and he slashed at his neck, hoping he wasn't going to tear his own neck apart with the enthusiasm. Cyn latched onto the wound without hesitating, without asking what he was supposed to do. Gabriel knew from having talked to others—demons and humans who'd bonded, including Cyn's cousin—that it was intuition and instinct, and even though Cyn didn't have a mate because he was a demon, he could feel the bond pulsing between them, waiting for them to complete it.

So they did. Gabriel tried to focus on the wound in Cyn's neck, licking it closed. He knew that if he shifted his attention to his neck and the way Cyn was lapping at it, he'd come before it was the right time.

Then Cyn lightly bit down, and Gabriel decided that he didn't care when he came, as long as he did.

He moved his hips, urging Cyn to push harder and faster. Cyn obeyed, and Gabriel realized he didn't need him to. Cyn was done drinking his blood, He could tell—they both could—the exact moment the bond between them swelled and clicked into place. Gabriel didn't have to focus or think about his grandma in her underwear. He didn't need to stop himself from coming, and he couldn't have, even if he'd wanted to.

He didn't.

What he'd been told was true. The pleasure intensified, and as he and Cyn both came almost in unison, it looped, giving Gabriel the sensation of the strongest orgasm that he'd ever had — and the longest one.

Gabriel wasn't sure how long he and Cyn stayed locked like that, wrapped around each other, their pleasure feeding into and from the bond. When it was done, Cyn flopped on top of him, pushing the air out of his lungs. Gabriel needed that air, though, so he rolled Cyn off him and tried to breathe.

"Sorry," Cyn mumbled. He reached for his neck and poked at it, wincing.

He was probably sore, just like Gabriel, although Gabriel's neck wasn't the only part of him that hurt. "Your dick is too big," he complained.

Cyn laughed and hooked an arm around Gabriel's waist. "That's not what you were saying fifteen minutes ago."

"Maybe not, but I also didn't expect to come for, like, half an hour straight."

"I'm pretty sure that didn't last more than five minutes, hon."

"That's still too long." Gabriel's balls felt empty and as sore as his hole. He didn't even want to *think* about sex right now.

Cyn snuggled against him and sighed, his body utterly relaxed. "I'm glad you gave in and bit me."

"I couldn't say *no*. You're convincing."

"I was counting on that, although I think I have to continue working on it."

"You're only saying that because I said no to moving in together."

"For now." Cyn sounded upbeat, as he should. They both knew Gabriel wasn't going to continue saying no.

Cyn had a job now. He worked with Oliver, and while Gabriel had no idea how motors were supposed to work, he trusted Oliver when he said Cyn was good at what he did.

That meant that Cyn was earning a nice salary, and while he liked living with his cousin, Gabriel knew he was itching for a place of his own. The only reason he hadn't found one yet was that he thought it would be stupid for him to move out only to have to do it again once he and Gabriel moved in together. He wasn't wrong, but Gabriel wasn't sure he was ready to leave Alice.

Things with her were still tense. After Gabriel and Cyn had come back from that disaster of an arranged wedding, Gabriel had torn into Alice. He'd risked losing Cyn only because she'd let her grudge take over, and when he thought about it, he was still pissed. He also didn't understand her animosity, even after Oliver had gently pointed out that she was jealous and scared. He wasn't about to kick her out or turn his back on her because he'd found his mate. She ought to know that, and it hurt that she didn't.

"You need to forgive her," Cyn murmured.

Gabriel huffed. "How did you know I was thinking about Alice?"

Cyn tapped the tip of Gabriel's nose. "You got that fierce expression you always get when you think about her. Also, I can feel that you're frustrated, angry, and sad, and she's the only one that can create that mix of emotions in you."

Gabriel sighed. "I don't get how you managed to forgive her after what she did and said to you."

Cyn shrugged. "She apologized, and I do understand where she was coming from. You were her only family for so long, she was afraid to lose you, and for things to change. And they *are* changing. You can't deny that." He stroked a finger along the wound in Gabriel's neck and arched a brow.

He was right. Things were changing. Alice had gone to talk to Kameron, and the alpha was going to help her pay for her degree. That meant that Gabriel had been able to leave his job at the shelter, and he now limited himself to volunteering there. And *that* gave him more time to spend with Cyn.

He sighed. "I'm trying."

"I know." And it was almost easy to do when he and Cyn got downstairs for something to eat and found that Alice had cooked breakfast and was waiting for them.

It would take time for things to be okay with her again, but they were both working toward that, and that was what mattered.

Gabriel took her hand and squeezed before turning to dump pancakes on Cyn's plate, and when he faced Alice again, she was smiling—hesitantly, but smiling, nonetheless.

He smiled back.

YOU MAY ALSO ENJOY THE FOLLOWING FROM EXTASY BOOKS INC:

A Blessing in Disguise
Catherine Lievens

Excerpt

Dryden hated this. He didn't want to have to guide Rochester's guests to the back room. He didn't want to stand there while they bit drugged and terrified humans. He didn't want to have to leave the near-death humans there once the assholes were done eating them.

But he had to.

He'd gone against Rochester last time, and it hadn't ended well for him. As much as he hated not being able to help, he had to choose between them and himself, and this time, the choice was easy—almost too easy. It made him uncomfortable with himself, but he'd learned to ignore that kind of feelings a long time ago.

Dryden wished he could go back to the party, even though it meant he'd have to go around offering glasses of blood. At least he wouldn't have to listen to the whimpers and moans of pain.

"That was a good one," the woman he'd brought to the back room said as she rose.

She'd been straddling one of the male human's lap, and while she'd sounded like she'd enjoyed the position and the biting, he hadn't. His eyes were wide and glassy, and he reached for Dryden, but Dryden looked away.

He hated this. He wanted to help, but he couldn't.

The woman pushed her red hair behind her back and slunk toward Dryden. Dryden tensed, already knowing what was going to happen. Some vampires mixed feeding and sex as easily as if the two belonged in the same situation. Dryden supposed he might have done that, too, if he hadn't been turned in the circumstances he'd been turned in. But for him, life as a vampire had always been about blood and pain, not pleasure, and that would never change.

No matter how many beautiful women tried to get into his pants.

She stopped in front of Dryden and ran a finger down his chest, pulling the collar of his shirt to the side. He reached up and pushed it back, but she wasn't having any of it. She slipped a fingertip under the shirt and fingered the thick scar that was there, just under his collarbone. It made Dryden shiver, and not in a good way, both because of the memory the scar brought up and because he didn't want this woman to touch him.

Dryden stepped back. "I'll make sure you get back to the party safely."

The woman arched a brow. "Safely? Why, do you think someone is going to attack me on the way back?"

"Of course not." But Rochester didn't want any of his guests left alone in his house. He didn't trust them, just like they didn't trust him.

She pouted. "I'm not going to be able to convince you to have fun with me?"

She could have forced Dryden if she'd wanted to. He was surprised she wasn't, but he supposed not everyone Rochester knew was an asshole. That didn't make this woman a good person, but she could be worse. Or maybe she was worse but

Dryden didn't know it because she was being nice in this situation.

He didn't care, and he didn't want to find out.

He stepped to the side so she could walk ahead. "Please, after you," he murmured, slightly bowing. He hated these signs of submission, but by now, they were ingrained in him and came almost naturally. Rochester had been training him in this ever since he'd turned him into a vampire.

Dryden shuddered when he thought it should have been Morgan in his place. Morgan had always been the strongest one of them both, at least mentally, but things would have been so much worse for him if Dryden hadn't taken his place. Rochester hadn't wanted him only as a slave like he was using Dryden. No, he'd wanted Morgan for his body, because Morgan was small and had long hair and Rochester had wanted him in his bed since the first time he'd seen him. Rochester hadn't been married to Lucia back then, so no one would have stopped him.

Dryden had. He still didn't know why Rochester had agreed to the exchange. He'd wanted Morgan, and Morgan had been the one who'd snuck into his house and had stolen from him, not knowing that he was opening their lives up for something much more dangerous than cops and the law. Dryden didn't know why, but even after the years — decades — of torture, he was glad he Rochester had.

"What's your name?" the woman asked.

"My name doesn't matter."

She arched a brow. "It doesn't matter, huh? I bet Rochester doesn't want you to say it. Am I right?"

She was. Dryden had never found out why, but Rochester had made sure he knew not to tell anyone who he was and the history they shared.

"I'll take your non-answer as a no." She frowned. "Hey, are you—"

"Auriel. Are you monopolizing my slave?" Rochester drawled.

Dryden hadn't even seen him, and he fucking hoped the man wouldn't think he'd been about to talk. Of course, even if he didn't think Dryden had, it didn't mean he wouldn't take the opportunity to torture him a little. The asshole lived to cause pain, and he particularly liked inflicting it on Dryden. Dryden often wondered if it was because he'd taken Morgan's place, allowing Morgan to slip from Rochester's hands. He had no doubt Rochester had been planning on somehow get Morgan anyway, but Morgan had disappeared right after Dryden had been taken, just like Dryden had ordered him to. Dryden had been surprised since Morgan hadn't been known for doing what Dryden wanted unless he wanted it to. He'd never taken orders well, and that was one of the reasons his life would have been hell if he'd been in Dryden's place right now.

Dryden slunk away, leaving Rochester to talk with the red-haired woman. He didn't want any part in their conversation, and the longest Rochester's attention was on someone else, the better it would be for him.

He went back to the back room to clean up the blood spills and to make sure the man Auriel had drunk from was okay. He was still slumped on the couch, but he was breathing, which was more than Dryden could say for some of the other humans in the room. He knew they'd all be dead by the end of the evening, though, so he steeled himself and ignored their cries for help as he made the room presentable again—Rochester's words, not his.

The chain that bound his ankles together didn't make things easy, and he had to shuffle around, but he was glad to have something to focus on. He had to make sure he didn't walk too fast because he'd end up on his face otherwise.

"What do you think you're doing?" Rochester asked from behind Dryden. There was a barely contained fury in his voice, and Dryden wasn't sure what he'd done to deserve it. Of course, he only had to breathe to make Rochester angry most days, but still.

"I'm cleaning up," he said, making sure not to look at Rochester.

"With Auriel."

"I brought her here, made sure she had what she wanted, and walked her back. That's all."

"She's curious about you."

"She tried to get me to fuck her."

The anger on Rochester's face faded a bit. "That's why she was asking questions?"

Dryden shrugged. "I don't know. She tried to get me to fuck her, and I said no. I don't know how she took it or why she wanted it, although she just fed, so it's probably just that I was the only man able to perform in the room." There was no way any of the humans there would have been able to get hard, even if they hadn't been drugged up to their eyeballs. They'd been fed on, and they were terrified. No one would want to have sex in those conditions.

Rochester didn't look one hundred percent convinced, but he nodded. "Good. Continue to do your job, and don't talk to the guests. Actually, why don't you stay here with the snacks and make sure they survive until the end of the party? Some of them don't look as fresh as they ought to."

Dryden tightened his hands into fists. He felt the urge to attack Rochester and tear his head off about five times a day, but he couldn't react to his words. "Of course," he said instead, hoping it would save his hide once the guests left.

He knew how unlikely that was, though.

ABOUT THE AUTHOR

Catherine lives in Italy, country of good food and hot men. She used to write fantasy as a child, but it was reading her first gay erotic romance novel that made her realize that that was what she really wanted to write.

After graduating from college in English language and translation, she divides her day between writing, reading, taking care of her son and reading some more.

You can find her on Facebook and Twitter or on her website: authorcatherinelievens.wordpress.com

Email: lievens.catherine@gmail.com

Newsletter: http://eepurl.com/c-uvKn

www.ingramcontent.com/pod-product-compliance
Lightning Source LLC
Chambersburg PA
CBHW060634130626
46555CB00002B/805